TO BEDEVIL A DUKE

Lords of London, Book 1

TAMARA GILL

COPYRIGHT

DEDICATION

For my family. Always.

CHAPTER 1

London, 1805

Lady Darcy de Merle was foxed. A most scandalous and terrible way to be at her own ball, but the ratafia was quite delicious this evening, and surely she could be excused for imbibing more than she ought when celebrating the one-year anniversary of her husband's death and her relaunch into London Society.

Darcy looked down at her golden silk gown with small puffed sleeves. The empire cut accentuated her small waist and ample bosom enough to garner many admiring glances from the opposite sex. Her dark locks were pulled up into an intricate motif atop her head, and small loose curls fell about her face, softening the look. The pairing of golden gown and dark hair complemented her, and for the first time in years, she felt attractive.

Her departed husband, the Earl of Terrance, had never made her feel so. He was not missed, and it had taken all of Darcy's good breeding to wait out the twelve months required for mourning. Especially when she would

1

never mourn such a man. On his death, he'd left her nothing, which she had expected. Not that it impacted her very much. Her grandfather, having loved her most out of all his female grandchildren, had left her the London townhouse along with a very tidy sum should she ever require it. Darcy had been named for her grandfather, and had chosen to once again be known by his name from the day she'd placed her husband into the cold earth. Her father, the Earl de Merle, had supported her in her choice. Having been witness to her husband's indiscretions, his vile temper and cutting tongue, he was happy she reverted to the name she was born with, not the one given to her upon marriage.

It wasn't to be borne for a de Merle to be treated so shabbily, and as such, Darcy had clasped her freedom upon his death and would not look back. Life was to be lived, and she would never exist again under the atrocious circumstances she'd endured with Terrance.

The Viscountess Oliver and Darcy's dearest friend, came to stand with her. "You look positively decadent in that golden gown Darcy, and you know it. Your husband would have a seizure if he knew you were holding one of London's biggest balls in honor of the anniversary of his death, and your debut back into Society."

Darcy smiled in welcome. Fran was a tall, lithe woman with the most beautiful auburn hair, a trait from her Scottish roots. It amused Darcy that her husband, a man she should never have married in the first place, would be insulted by her actions. Oh, how she'd love to see his fat, ruddy cheeks blossom in annoyance and anger at her defiance of him. "How wonderful that sounds. But you know, as a woman renowned for scandal, I could not allow such an opportunity to pass. One must keep up the standard to which they intend to live. If I did not, that would be a scandal in itself."

Fran linked their arms and walked them along the outer edge of the ballroom floor. "You smell of wine. How much have you had this evening?"

"Enough that I know I should have no more, and I promise I will not." Although Darcy loved nothing more than scandalizing the ton, she would only ever go so far, and never crossed the invisible line that even her family's name could not redeem her from. Two years into her marriage she'd decided that she would no longer live as a doormat to her husband, and had begun attending parties again, dancing and flirting her way about London. Her husband did not approve, would bellow and break furniture and valuables, but Darcy had had enough. If she could not divorce the man, she would at least live her own life, just as he did.

"The last thing you want is to be compromised by a money-hungry rake, looking to catch you at your most vulnerable," Fran said. "Unless of course you wish to be married again."

Darcy gasped. "Not in a million years, Lady Oliver. The last thing that I want is another husband. Although now that I'm free from Terrance, I may look for a lover."

It was her friend's turn to gasp before she grinned, just as she used to when they were young women at Mrs. Dew's Finishing School for Young Ladies in Bath, before they were about to sneak off and have some fun that the teachers were never aware of.

"There are many gentlemen here this evening who'd be only too happy to oblige you, I'm sure."

Darcy looked about. There were a few gentlemen looking her way, some nodding slightly, others giving the best smouldering look they knew how to perform. And maybe one of these men would do. Certainly, Mr. Ambrose could prove useful. That he was a wealthy American and would not be staying long could be a point in his favour. A lover this Season was paramount for her happiness and sanity, if she were honest.

Not that her friend Fran knew, but Darcy had attended a masked ball one evening that opened her eyes to the pleasures women could have. She hadn't participated, merely skulked about drinking champagne, but many others were more than happy to explore, and become better acquainted with the opposite sex within only a matter of hours.

As Darcy was fetching her cloak, ready to leave, she overheard a woman that sounded to be behind the cloak rooms' door, making sounds unlike anything she'd ever heard before. It had been one of ecstasy, of begging and gasping, and she'd wanted to know what it was that the woman adored so. How did a man make a woman react in such a way? Her late husband had never fulfilled her needs, and by the time he passed away they'd not shared a bed for a year or more.

"What do you think of Mr. Ambrose?" Darcy asked, taking two glasses of champagne from a passing footman, ignoring the fact she wasn't supposed to be having any more to drink.

"Delicious," Fran said, giggling. "Although please do not tell Lord Oliver I said such a thing. You know how he can be."

Only too well. Viscount Oliver, Fran's husband of two years, was devoted to her, and at times could be quite the jealous husband. Not that Fran would ever wish to leave him. They were, in Darcy's estimation, quite a lovable couple. Perfectly made for each other.

"I would never tease his lordship, so even if I wanted to

I would never go against your word. But I do think you're right. Mr. Ambrose would do very well pleasuring a woman, I think."

Fran barked out a scandalously unladylike laugh, which had those about them turn at the outburst. Darcy smiled as if she'd not shocked her friend into hysterics. "Do you not agree?"

"Pleasuring a woman? Darcy, you are too wild. Wherever did you hear such a saying?"

"I played whist with the stable hands yesterday evening, and after some beer, the men were quite free with their speech. I learnt quite a few sayings, if you wish to be enlightened?"

"Enlightened may be the wrong word to use in this case," Fran said, taking a sip of her champagne. "But in all truth, my dear, do you think you will take a lover?"

Darcy shrugged. Oh yes, she wanted a lover. To find pleasure in the arms of a man without having to tie herself to him indefinitely. "Maybe, if I find a gentleman that I want to sleep with." God knows her deceased husband Terrance had been terrible in bed, and she'd often been thankful he'd had his whores, if only to keep him away from her. He did not know anything about giving pleasure to a woman. It was like lying with a block of wood that grunted a lot and was finished within a minute.

Fran sighed as she watched her husband chatting with some other guests across the room. "It is so very important that they know how to please. I could not bear my marriage if I did not find my husband attractive in that sense. I am certainly blessed that Papa allowed me to choose someone I loved to marry, not some gentleman who'd bring fortune and prestige to our name."

"Lucky that Lord Oliver brought those things in any case, along with his heart for you."

"He did," Fran said, turning her gaze back to Darcy. "People will expect a de Merle to marry high, and many thought you did not marry to your station with the earl since his pockets were to let. What will you do?"

"I will do as I please, although in hindsight I probably should have listened to Papa when he said the man was a dandy. How very accurate he was in his estimation." Darcy sighed, thinking back on that time. "I feel for Papa, for he did not know Terrance was so deep in debt. As you know the man kept his money troubles well buried until after our marriage."

Not to mention her own blindness toward Terrance. To be so easily swayed by declarations of undying love, of a life that would be comfortable and happy, to believe whatever came out of his mouth as truth, was a mistake she'd not make again with another man. This time she would choose a man who shared her values, did not wish for marriage, and understood women's needs behind closed doors. And one who did not expect her to finance his lifestyle.

"Yes, indeed." Fran smiled. "What about the Duke Athelby? Rumor has it he's seriously searching for a wife, and he's dreadfully handsome. Dark and brooding, tall, and with that slight air of aloofness to all that's before him. I think he may pleasure you very well."

Darcy choked on her champagne at her friend's use of her words. She directed her attention to the duke. A shame she had given up any thoughts pertaining to the man, but then it was his own fault. No longer did Darcy de Merle go out of her way to please any man, especially one that thought all women should be seen and not heard, relegated to the nursery to produce babies. He was severe, and his words were sharp enough to cut even the thickest-skinned person among her set if he disliked their appearance or manner. The duke was a towering terror that made most debutantes shudder in their silk slippers, and gentlemen walk with care.

Not Darcy though.

She'd merely dismissed him as a man who thought too much of himself, as he always had. Not a feature that was at all redeeming. That Darcy's godmother—his grandmother and only surviving relative—thought he held qualities that would suit her and other women was an absurd notion. He might be a gentleman, a duke even, but his manners—his lack of knowing when to speak and when to hold one's tongue—made it debatable. Women did not want to be chastised over what they wore, or how they ate, or who their friends were. The duke was only too willing to point out any little flaws if he deemed them so. Darcy shook her head. His grandmother seemed to think Athelby had a heart. How wrong she was.

It was really quite unfortunate that the woman was so completely blind.

"The duke is a no, I can promise you that. He's a young, handsome man until he opens his mouth, and then a grumpy, middle-aged man appears. It is no surprise to me he's not married, for who'd put up with such a displeasing creature?" Although he wasn't displeasing to the eye, her words were not as true as she'd wanted them to sound. Sometimes when he laughed, which wasn't often, she glimpsed the boy he'd once been in the man he'd become, and she longed to have him back.

"Creature may be too harsh a term, Darcy. Maybe his grandmother is right, and he's merely misunderstood."

Darcy shook her head, smiling at Fran. "You've always wanted to see the best of people, but sometimes it just isn't there. And I for one did not escape a marriage, a husband who treated me like a piece of dirt beneath his hessian boots, to merely marry another who would do the same. God forbid that my gown be a little too low cut, or that if I sat before a fire my ankles showed. The duke would have an apoplectic fit! I couldn't stand it, and you know papa would never survive seeing me married to another uptight prig."

Fran laughed just as her husband walked toward them, the grin on his face foretelling that he was here to claim his wife for the waltz that was due to start.

He bowed to Darcy and then Fran, taking his wife's hand before kissing it softly. "I believe the next dance is mine to claim, my dear."

Fran blushed. "I do believe you're right, my lord." Fran grinned over her shoulder as she walked away. "I will be back soon, my dear."

They walked off and joined the other couples that were congregating on the dance floor. Darcy watched them, and the others, as they started to glide through the graceful movements of the waltz. It was a dance she herself loved, but in her current situation, it was probably best that she hadn't been asked to engage in it. No one wanted to see a woman fall over due to her decidedly unstable foxed feet.

"I see you've consumed too much wine this evening," the Duke of Athelby said, startling her.

She smiled up at him, knowing just how well that would annoy him. "I have, and how liberating it is. And you should probably consider yourself fortunate that I am a little foxed."

"And why is that, Lady de Merle…if that is what you're calling yourself these days."

"Why yes, it is. And you do know, Duke, that you're standing next to a widowed woman, someone who has been used, and is not as perfect as we all know you're fond of. Maybe it wouldn't be wise for a man with such stellar manners and an impeccable reputation to be doing such a scandalous thing."

"I'm sure I shall survive, even though your vulgar ball, which is being held exactly twelve months to the day since your husband's funeral, is far from appropriate. I fear such a move will limit the time my grandmother may spend with you in the foreseeable future. I cannot have her reputation tarnished in such a way."

Darcy narrowed her eyes. "Tarnished? You are trying to make me laugh, yes? How absurd that a woman of your grandmother's age would even be worried about her reputation. Are you sure that the real reason you don't want her around me is due to your narrowed views on life?"

The muscle in his jaw worked, always a sign he was fighting to remain civil. Keeping his temper was not something the Duke of Athelby was famous for. Darcy studied his profile, his strong jaw and straight nose. The man was devastatingly handsome, his features severe and powerful. There was a time, when they were both still children, that she had been determined to marry him. He'd been carefree then, as wild and boisterous as herself, and for the month-long house party that their parents had attended, to which they had been brought along, they had been inseparable. It was years before they met again, and by then Cameron had come into his title and the fun-loving, incorrigible, laughing boy that she'd known was gone.

"It is my wish for the connection to be severed somewhat. It is for the best. You must see that," he said with an arrogant lift of his head.

Darcy spotted his grandmother strolling their way and smiled in welcome. "Ah, I see Lady Ainsworth is here. Maybe we can ask her about your new rules."

Athelby sputtered but didn't have time to divert his grandmother before Darcy took the older woman's arm and led her over to a settee near an unlit hearth. The duke followed, and Darcy did her best to ignore his black scowl. The viscountess kissed Darcy on the cheek and kept her hands firmly clasped in her own.

"How is my dear, dear goddaughter? I hope you're enjoying yourself this evening?"

"I am, my lady, very much so, but I've just had the most distressing news." Darcy looked up at Athelby, his steely gaze locked on her. It did odd things to her stomach having his attention in such a way. She turned her attention back to Lady Ainsworth to escape it.

"Your grandson has just informed me tonight that our association must come to an end."

"Now, those were not my exact words—"

Her ladyship held up her hand, halting her grandson's explanation. "What did he say, my dear? You have my full attention," she said, casting an irritated glance at Athelby.

"Due to my husband's death, and holding this ball twelve months to the day since we laid Terrance to rest, the duke believes that I would only bring shame and ruination to your family should we be seen together. This ball is a garish act and one that casts me in the light of a woman who did not love her husband." Not that she had at all, but her ladyship didn't need to know that. "And so, we must part from this night on. Never to be seen together again, I'm afraid."

"Your sarcasm is not lost on me, Lady de Merle," the duke said, glaring to the point that his brows almost joined, and not caring who in the upper ten-thousand saw it.

Darcy wanted him to be aware of her annoyance, and although she smiled sweetly at Lady Ainsworth, what the duke had said earlier was not to be borne. How dare he make her feel like she was the one who'd done something wrong. That her conduct was somehow worse than her husband's whoring and gambling, most of which was with her money. Another little prickle in her soul was that she'd had to walk away from Terrance's London home, a house she'd rightfully saved from being taken back by the bank upon his death. How could she not celebrate being rid of a complete fool? She would not pretend to have a broken heart, or to be a sad little widow.

"Well, that is absurd, and I can assure you, my dear," Lady Ainsworth said, her jowls shaking a little in wrath, "I will be spending just as much time with you as I always have. Your mama was one of my closest friends, no matter the twenty-year difference between us. I promised her that I would care for you until the day I died, and I will not, no matter what my grandson has to say about it, deviate from the honor."

"Thank you, Your Ladyship."

"Grandmother, see sense. If I'm to find a wife of similar standards to my own, surely you can see that our family being associated with a renowned hellion, a woman who flaunts her freedom from the marriage state with little care for her reputation, would not show us in a favourable light," he said, beyond frustrated.

Lady Ainsworth sighed, looking down her nose at her grandson. Not the easiest of feats considering his grace was standing, and both Darcy and her ladyship were sitting. "I will not hear of such stupidity again. Really, Cameron, do step off that high horse you seem so acquainted with these days and return to our level."

Darcy's lips twitched, and she fought not to giggle at the reddening of his grace's cheeks. Really, he was being silly looking down on her so. "What if I promise that whenever I'm around her ladyship, and yourself for that matter, I will be on my best behavior?" she said, taking pity on the man. If it meant she could continue socializing with

Lady Ainsworth, she would take care. When she decided to enjoy her Season and all the opportunities this and others might bring, she never meant to inadvertently hurt others. If his association with her would hurt his chances of making a match, then she would behave herself while around him.

"You're around us tonight, and yet you're foxed. Not that my grandmother has noticed such a thing."

"Oh, for pity's sake, it is a ball, and one that is being hosted by me. I may drink if I wish, and I'll not have even a duke tell me what to do."

"That is enough, both of you," her ladyship said, casting them both a dark glance. "Anyone listening would think you're a bickering married couple already, like so many around us. Your Grace, you do not have the right to be so opinionated about someone who has been a family friend for many years. You need to remember that if you cannot say anything nice, you do not say anything at all."

"I think, Grandmother, that is the first logical thing you've said this evening. It is also my cue to leave." He bowed. "Good evening, ladies," he said, heading in the direction of the ballroom doors.

Darcy growled, throwing daggers at his back as he made his way through the ton. Argh, the man was infuriating and so high and mighty. She had equally good breeding—she was a de Merle. How dare he look down his nose at her.

"Darcy, my dear. I know your mind is no doubt coming up with multiple ways of getting back at my grandson, but please let him be. I'm hoping that when he gets a wife, his emotional wall and his rather cutting opinions may abate a little."

"I doubt that they will, but I promise I shall not cause trouble for him," Darcy said. "We differ in opinions, and no doubt will again. I will not stop inviting him to events or talking to him should our paths cross."

"Thank you, my dear."

Her ladyship paused, a small frown line between her brows the only indication that she was concerned about the duke. Otherwise Lady Ainsworth was a very attractive woman for her age. Of course she had smile lines, and her hair was grey, but otherwise, time had been very kind to her.

"I think my grandson is lonely. And I do believe that is why he's so angry at the world. He spent his formative years with no one to argue, play, and share secrets with. The brothers had an age gap of over ten years, they hardly knew one another. He's grown so used to his own company that I think he finds it hard to socialize. As was demonstrated this evening."

A pang of sadness tweaked inside Darcy at the memory of the carriage accident that had taken the life of the duke's elder brother. But remembering his ungentlemanly words, she tried to push aside any inclination to feel sorry for the duke. Not very successfully, however. "I'm sure you're right, Lady Ainsworth. A happy union is just what his grace needs, and maybe this will be the Season that he finds a woman to warm his bed."

"Sometimes I think you're the perfect person for Cameron. You both certainly have a wicked tongue," her ladyship said, a calculating twinkle in her blue orbs.

Darcy chuckled, waving a footman over to bring them champagne. "We would not suit, and I'm not looking to marry anyone. Marriage to Lord Terrance was quite enough for one lifetime."

Her ladyship sighed, taking a small sip of her champagne. "Well, that is a shame, for I would love to have you as a granddaughter as well as my goddaughter. But," she said, a sad tilt to her lips, "one cannot have everything that they wish. I often fret that I shall never see the two people I care for most happy and settled in the world."

Darcy took her ladyship's hand and squeezed. She was not immune to her words, that often sparked guilt within her. And knowing it was completely on purpose on her ladyship's behalf made her smile. "Do behave, Godmother. I know what game you're playing, and once again, his grace and myself do not suit. My only connection to the gentleman is through you, and that is where it shall stay. As stated previously tonight, and many times at previous events, if you recall."

"One must try to make you understand, my dear. It never hurts to plant a suggestion in someone's mind, for it to germinate and possibly make them wonder if it has merit."

"You're incorrigible," Darcy said, laughing.

"I know," her ladyship replied, no remorse whatsoever in her tone.

Darcy looked back at the duke and tried to imagine him in her bed. He was certainly one of the most striking, powerful men in London. In the throes of passion, wild and wicked, maybe he would look even more so. He turned and looked down at Miss Watson, whom he was currently conversing with, frowning and looking as though he was chastising the poor woman. Darcy shook her head. No, he would never do.

His grace looked up and their gazes smashed together. The pit of her stomach clenched and her cheeks flushed from the inspection he bestowed on her. What a shame she disliked him so much. Or was he like his grandmother said —merely misunderstood?

CHAPTER 2

Cameron, Duke of Athelby strolled down Bond Street, his cane tapping a beat on the cobbled foot-path as he went. People moved out of his way, a common occurrence for him and a helpful one. A few debutants that he'd seen the previous evening at Almacks tittered as their mama bade him a good day. Without stopping and only giving the slightest bow, Athelby continued. Weston's, his tailor, was not much further, and he didn't have time to stop. The new cravats he had ordered last week were not to his standard and became limp halfway through events, and it was not to be borne. He would need to speak with Weston himself, to have the situation remedied. His clothes, along with his reputation, must always be of the highest standard.

No one would ever describe the Duke of Athelby as a man without respect for himself or his name. Never would he allow scandal to tarnish his title again. If his late brother had taught him anything, it was that the family name and what the ducal title meant to people must never be taken for granted. Never used or abused for a life of reckless follies.

His step faltered and he almost dropped his cane when Lady Darcy de Merle, as she was calling herself these days, stepped out of a fabric emporium laughing at something her ladies' maid said. He frowned. Who laughed with their servants? Really, the woman had no shame.

He studied her as she continued her conversation. Darcy was striking, with ebony locks and the darkest, longest lashes he'd ever seen on a woman. Her lips were full, but not overly so. On her coming out she'd been married before the Season's end, and his one regret was never having danced with her. They had been friends once, a long time ago, but a lot had happened since then.

She caught sight of him, and her features shuttered. He ignored the pang of regret that darted through him. It was such a pity to see the smile that had lit her beautiful face fall from view. She curtsied—the shallowest he'd ever seen—as he bowed.

"Your Grace," she said. Or spat more like, as if the word was toxic on her tongue.

"Lady de Merle. I see you're quite recovered from your exertions last evening."

She stared at him a moment, and he had the oddest urge to shift on his feet. An absurd notion, since he'd done nothing wrong. He'd merely pointed out that it was she who had been foxed last evening and made a fool of herself. And after such inebriation, it was quite common for the person inflicted to be ill the following day. Or so he'd heard. He never partook in such pastimes. On top of being morally well-behaved, he also did not drink. Just the thought of having to cast up his accounts was enough to halt any such thoughts, if he had any. Which he had not.

"I am, and what wonderful exertions they were, Your

Grace. But I'm sure, with your stoic way of life, you would not know what I'm talking about."

He clamped his jaw as annoyance tinged her tone, trying to curb his irritation that she'd made a total fool of herself the previous evening. Women should not be foxed —it wasn't becoming, and certainly not for an earl's daughter. She would never fit his mould of duchess. No wife of his would indulge to excess, gossip, or act without decorum. No matter how beautiful she may be, even now looking up at him with eyes that could bewitch the strongest man, Darcy de Merle would not do. Ever.

"I do not, no." He glanced toward the shop from which Darcy had exited and quickly looked away when he spied a woman inside twirling before mirrors and her admirers. They really ought to put up curtains to stop the passing public from seeing such a thing.

"What a shame, Your Grace," Darcy said, waving down a hackney cab like a commoner. "For if you tried a little fun, you might just have some. Good day."

Athelby gaped at her but shut his mouth with a snap when he realized Darcy and her maid were laughing at him.

He walked on, not bothering to wait for her hackney to pull away. To think that his grandmother would like that piece of muslin to be his wife was an absurd notion. And she'd had many absurd notions over the years when trying to matchmake him with some preening miss new to town.

No one so far had met his exacting standards, and in all honesty, it was becoming a problem. He was no longer the young man he had been—within a few months he would turn nine and twenty. He was well due to settle down and beget some heirs.

He didn't want to lower his expectations, and yet...a wife was proving hard to acquire. His brother, God rest his soul, never had trouble with women, and it was a carriage race over a woman, his betrothed no less, that had taken his life. Although Athelby had only been young when his brother had passed away, the pain of his death had wrecked his mother and father, which was something he would never have inflicted on them.

There were women who'd turned their gazes his way, but he'd simply directed his in the opposite direction. None of them had been suitable. The ones he had courted always proved, eventually, that they would not suit. Their laughs were grating, or they were too skittish around a duke, or not skittish enough. They gossiped too much or hung about him with an air of desperation he could never abide.

He wanted a woman similar to him. One who played by the rules, spoke only when required, and did not enter into the games of the ton. Surely such a woman was not impossible to find.

The image of Darcy laughing at him, her mischievous nature that had once been the sole focus of his life—at least for the month-long house party they had attended as children—taunted him. He'd thought her perfect, and fun, not something he thought a girl could be. She'd not lost that love of life, but instead of admiring her for such a view, all it did was vex him.

Disregarding his cravats entirely, he went to White's and was soon ensconced in the first-floor sitting room. He accepted a copy of the *Times* from a footman and started to read the latest political dramas to keep his mind from wandering to the vexing Darcy who aggravated him to no end.

The leather chair across from him groaned as someone sat down, and Athelby wanted to growl at the interruption. He was not of the mind to have another conversation that

TO BEDEVIL A DUKE

would probably be as annoying as the last one he'd had on Bond Street.

"Your Grace," a deep, familiar voice said from behind his paper.

Hunter, or the Marquess of Aaron as the ton knew him, was probably the only gentleman in the ton Athelby called a friend. "Aaron, I did not think Thursday was your day for White's."

"It is not, but there is a thousand pounds up for grabs due to a bet which I could not pass up."

Aaron loved gambling, and no matter how many times Athelby lectured his friend on the pitfalls, the stupidity and dangers of gambling, he chose not to listen and continued to squander his family's fortune. Not that the man didn't have more than enough to last him ten lifetimes. However any such waste was really not appropriate.

"Are you not going to ask me what the bet is about?"

Athelby lowered his paper and gave his friend his full attention. "Even though I do not care, I'm sure you're going to tell me in any case."

"I thought the bet would interest you since it involves your family."

"My family!" Athelby sat up, closed his paper, and placed it on the table before him. "What on earth could a bet here at White's have to do with us?" His mind raced as to what it could possibly be about.

Aaron laughed, sitting back in his chair as if it was a lark to see him so addled.

"Well, not really your family, but certainly a close friend of yours and your grandmother's goddaughter," he grinned.

Darcy. "What are they betting on her ladyship this time?" Not that he wanted to know, but still, with the knowledge of what was happening here, he had reason to speak to Lady de Merle and try to correct her manners so that not one of these gentlemen would win such a sum. It was not to be borne.

"They're betting that sweet piece of muslin will be married before the end of the Season. Or have a lover. I should say there are two bets, five hundred pounds apiece —one for marriage, one for a lover."

The notion of Darcy taking a lover made him want to be physically ill. He blinked to clear his vision of her enjoying a man using the carnal knowledge she had gained from marriage. He'd never admit it to anyone, but the day she'd announced her betrothal to the Earl of Terrance something had died within Athelby, curled up and rotted away. Not that she had ever been meant for him. It had never been that way between them. Friends yes, lovers never. It was simply irritation that she had managed to accomplish something that he had not.

That was all it was. Nothing more.

The little devil now sitting on his shoulder snickered and whispered *liar* in his ear, and he flicked a piece of lint from his coat.

"And you're going to add your name to this bet?" Athelby met his friend's amused glance with a narrowed gaze.

"I am and so should you. You know her better than most. I bet should you ask her she may even tell you her choice. For it is rumored she's looking for a lover, and it would be a fool indeed who turned down that little fox."

Athelby clenched his fists and reminded himself that Lord Aaron was his friend. "If she asks you to be her lover, I would hope *you* would turn her down."

Ire flashed in his eyes before he crossed his long legs before the table between them. "Absolutely not! I'm not a simpleton."

The words hit Athelby, another blow to his gut or possibly a little higher. What was wrong with him? It was certainly not jealousy, although the emotion he was experiencing was eerily similar to it. Whatever it was, he would mention it to his doctor at his next appointment, which occurred weekly. One should not ignore their health, and being a duke without an heir, keeping healthy was paramount.

The thought of being jealous of who took Darcy de Merle to her bed was a ridiculous notion and not something any sane man would consider.

"As she's my grandmother's goddaughter, I would hope because of our friendship you would indeed say no to an affair with the lady, and help prevent any trouble she could find herself in should she sleep with a man not her husband."

Aaron sighed, nodding slowly. "I see your predicament, and it's to your credit that you're worried about her. But men of our ilk know how to ensure no unexpected gift is bestowed and delivered several months later."

"You cannot guarantee that, and she would indeed be ruined if that befell her. I ask again, as your friend, do not try to seduce Darcy. She is not for you."

"Who is she for then, shall I ask?" His friend steepled his fingers before his chin and watched him with eyes that could read a blank page, Athelby was certain. "You, by chance?"

"Certainly not," he protested with a laugh, but the sound came out hollow, and that little devil again whispered *liar* in his ear. "I cannot tolerate her wayward manners or flagrant disregard for rules and manners within our society. Sometimes I despair that she is even of noble blood."

"Oh, but you forget who her family is and their strong-willed, proud heritage. The de Merles are not people who can be told what to do. They make the rules that the rest of us should follow. If we don't, we're left out in the cold and soon forgotten."

How very true. It had always surprised Athelby that Darcy seemed to be able to do and say whatever she pleased without ever receiving censure from society. It was almost as if the family were immune to the repercussions of their scandalous pursuits.

"Well, I would be quite happy to be left behind if it meant not living the life that Darcy de Merle seems determined to inhabit." Athelby stood, and straightened his jacket. "I bid you good day."

"Shall I see you at my sister's ball this evening? You know it's her first since marrying the Earl of Glenn, and Sara has always been fond of you."

"I sent my response directly after receiving the invitation. I shall be in attendance."

Aaron grinned. "Very good. See you this evening then, Your Grace."

Athelby left White's. Thankfully his coachman had followed him on his jaunt and was parked out front, so he was able to leave directly. He tapped on the roof with his cane and stared sightlessly out the window. Why did the thought of Darcy moving on with her life, loving someone else and possibly marrying another gentleman, annoy him so much?

He called out the window for his coachman to take him to the residence of Dr. Duncan, his physician. He needed to see his doctor posthaste. There wasn't a moment to lose, for there was certainly something wrong with him. And the name of this disease was Darcy de Merle.

DARCY, and her friend Lady Oliver, had enjoyed their evening so far at the Earl and Countess of Glenn's first official ball since being married at the end of last Season. Darcy had always been fond of Sara and was delighted she'd made a love match with Lord Glenn, who'd always been kind and amiable to others.

One person Darcy didn't particularly wish to see was unfortunately across the room, although tonight he seemed a little out of sorts.

She studied the Duke of Athelby as he spoke to the hosts and the countess' brother, the Marquess of Aaron. The duke held a tumbler of what looked to be brandy, and the notion he would consume such a beverage gave her pause.

"I can see who you're looking at, and I can also see the clock within your mind ticking over as to why he's drinking," Fran said.

"Do you think it's whisky he's drinking?" Darcy had to admit that seeing him throw it back and ask for a refill left her positively astounded.

"It is a little odd, to say the least. Maybe he's trying to be more like his peers, although I doubt that would be the case. Everyone knows how much he detests gambling, drunkenness, and inappropriate behavior."

Hmm. Darcy watched him for a little while longer before a throng of beaux bowed before her during the next few hours and she was swept away into waltzing and cotillions, and all thoughts of the duke were forgotten.

That was until some hours later, when she walked out onto the terrace to find the Duke of Athelby bent over the balustrade, groaning.

"Athelby, can I be of assistance? You do not look very well, your grace."

He cringed noting her presence. "I'm mortified to say

that you've come across me, Lady de Merle, in a state of inebriation. What a hypocrite you must think me."

Darcy smiled, and even though she was certainly thinking it, she wouldn't tease him about the fact right now. He really did seem quite ill. "It's actually a relief to see you such. I had thought for some time that you weren't human."

He barked out a laugh and then groaned. "I'm human, I promise you." His words were slurred, and the duke looked anything but ducal right at this moment. "I know you think I'm a pompous fool. A man who thinks too highly of himself."

Darcy met his gaze. "I won't lie to you since we were friends as children, but yes, I do think that sometimes. But I also wonder why. You never used to be like that, Cameron."

It seemed that her use of his given name wasn't missed by him, even in his foxed condition. Surprisingly he took her hand, idly playing with her fingers. "If anyone saw me now they'd think I was my brother. The drunken fool who couldn't hold his liquor."

"You don't talk of Marcus very often. And you do yourself a discredit, Your Grace. You're nothing like your brother."

He sighed, running his other hand through his hair. "I fear that with only the smallest coaxing I could turn into him. And where would that leave the title, my home, and tenants who rely on me?"

"You are foxed. That will not make you your brother. And anyway," she said, placing her hand over his that continued to clasp hers. "What was so wrong with being like your sibling? I only vaguely remember him, but the times we did meet I never thought him an ogre."

"He was my brother, and I loved him, but I refuse to

follow him into an early grave." Cameron groaned and, turning toward the gardens, retched all over Lady Glenn's roses.

He waved her away, but instead of leaving, Darcy pulled his white handkerchief out of his coat pocket and handed it to him.

The duke took it and wiped his mouth before groaning and dropping his head as he sat on the stone balustrade.

"When I'm better I will kill the Marquess. Aaron stated it was merely a new punch that Lady Glenn's cook had created. I will not forgive the man his duplicity."

Darcy rubbed along his grace's shoulders and ignored the fact that beneath her hand was a very firm, muscular man, more so than she'd thought. She pushed aside the thought of what he'd look like without his shirt and instead said, "I shall fetch you some water. I will be right back." After hearing his fears of turning out like his brother, she couldn't help but feel for the man. In his quest to be the perfect duke, he'd become a man who never relaxed, who no longer knew how to live, even in moderation.

She did as she promised and within a few minutes returned to where she had left his grace, only to find him missing.

"I am here," he said, the slurred voice sounding from behind her.

She looked about then went and sat next to him in the small alcove that was situated between two windows. The rooms were not lit, and not in use this evening, so they were kept hidden. Probably a fortunate thing considering his grace was not very well. Should anyone catch him in such a state, the gossip that would befall him would not be easy for the man to take. Such a stickler for proper manners, he could not bear to be seen as anything other than what he preached. And after tonight, she understood a little as to why that was. His grandmother had tried to tell her in her way, but it wasn't until Cameron had explained that Darcy understood him better.

"Drink this, but only in sips. It should make you feel better."

He took the glass and did as she bade, not saying a word, merely sitting there like a lost little boy. Although he didn't look like a boy at all. In fact, the disarray Darcy now saw him in—untied cravat, messy hair that was no longer suitably combed, and slightly bloodshot eyes—made him look wild, untamed, and nothing like she'd ever seen him before.

In fact, the duke in this unkempt state was exceptionally handsome.

"Please do not tell anyone of my state. I know we're not friends, but please, if you can do this one thing for me I'll be forever grateful."

Darcy turned her attention toward the garden, seemingly thinking over his grace's question, though she knew she would never tell of his shame. She might be a woman who enjoyed parties, dancing, and revelry, but she was not a snitch or a gossiper. And she could never make fun of a man who'd had a cruel joke played upon him.

She turned to look at him and a shiver stole over her when she found him staring at her. In this dark alcove, his grace seemed predatory, nothing like he normally was. It left her a little unsure and wary. Maybe it was she who'd had too much wine this evening.

"I will not tell a soul, ever. You have my word."

His grace sighed and leaned back against the house. "I feel dreadful. Is this normal? If so, I wonder why so many people indulge in such pastimes."

"You drank quite a few glasses, Your Grace, and in quick succession. It is no wonder that you do not feel well."

Darcy stood, holding out her hand to him. He took it and stood.

"Walk to the front of the house, and I shall have your carriage called at the same time as mine. Return home, keep drinking water, and get some sleep. You may have a megrim tomorrow, but you should start to feel better by the afternoon."

The duke took her hand, bending over it and kissing her gloved fingers lightly. "Thank you, Darcy."

It wasn't often he used her name. In fact, she couldn't remember the last time—maybe it was when they were thrown together as children. Again a shiver of awareness flowed through her, and she stepped back to break whatever absurdness was taking over her body.

"You're welcome, but go. Wait in the shadows and you will see your carriage soon enough. And may I suggest in future not to listen to Lord Aaron. You know how much he loves to have a laugh at others' expense."

"I do, and his lordship will have his comeuppance if it's the last thing I do."

Darcy smiled and left, doing what she promised. While waiting for her own carriage, she watched as his grace came from beside the house and stepped up into his vehicle. Again, she was reminded of how tall he was, his athletic form that she'd not noticed until tonight.

She sighed, wrapped her cloak tighter about her, stepped down the three steps from the house and climbed up into her own carriage, calling out the address for Sir Richard Walton's card party that she'd also been invited to. With her good deed done for this evening, it was still early, and more fun was to be had. And maybe, just maybe, luck would be on her side tonight and she would win a few hands instead of always donating her funds to others' deep pockets.

CHAPTER 3

D arcy did not see his grace at any events over the next several days. She put it down to the duke being embarrassed over what she'd seen him doing and the state of his dress and appearance. Not to mention what he'd told her of his brother, which in his inebriated state may not have been on purpose.

Now, after too long a time, Darcy wanted to see him—something she'd never thought to imagine—if only to see for herself that he had survived his night of drunkenness and was well again. Back to his normal self, insulting matrons and scaring the breeches off young bucks who acted without decorum. This evening she'd not even seen her godmother, whom she'd been told had returned to the family's country estate after coming down with a cold. Darcy would have to write her well on the morrow and wish for her speedy return.

Darcy's heart thumped when the master of ceremonies called out the Duke of Athelby. She turned to see his grace making his address to their hosts.

He searched the crowd as he walked through the

gathered throng before his gaze caught hers and did not shift. Darcy smiled at him, nodding slightly, and he in turn came toward her, the sea of people seemingly moving out of his way so his progress was swift and without incident.

Darcy curtsied, holding out her hand as he bowed, kissing her fingers slightly. "Lady de Merle. I hope I find you well this evening?"

"And I you, Your Grace."

Understanding dawned in his eyes and he laughed. Darcy stood mute for a moment. The duke had a wonderful, rich laugh. A laugh that lit up his eyes and changed his stoic look to one of animated delight.

Damn it all to hell.

"I am very well, and I promise to only drink non-spiked punch this evening."

She smiled. "You know, there is no crime in having whisky, champagne, or wine, Your Grace. As long as it is in moderation."

"And this from a woman who not a week ago was in her cups."

Disappointment stabbed at her that his grace's attitude had not changed. Here he was, back to his cutting jibes within five minutes of arriving at the ball.

"I may have been foxed, but I did not have the pleasure of regurgitating it like others are wont to do."

His jaw clenched. "Touché. I cede your point."

"I should think so."

Lord Aaron joined them and bowed before Darcy.

"I believe this next set is mine, Lady de Merle."

Darcy dipped into a curtsy before the duke, not missing his flash of annoyance that the marquess had asked her to dance. It sparked a little devil inside of her to play up to his lordship and irritate Athelby more than she ought.

"It is, my lord." Darcy took his hand and let him lead her to the dance floor as others set up to join in a quadrille.

The dance gave Darcy the opportunity to find out why the marquess had played such a trick on his friend. "Did you know that the punch you gave his grace last week was anything but punch, and was, in fact, some sort of beverage that made him foxed?"

The marquess grinned, laughter in his eyes. "I did know, but my sister's cook is very clever indeed, and anyone drinking the brew had no idea that too much of it would leave you in your cups."

"I thought you and the duke were friends. How could you let him get into such a state knowing he is against those sorts of vices?"

"Because," the marquess said, growing serious, "if he does not loosen up a little, see life for what it is, that it is to be lived and enjoyed, it will end with him a lonely, bitter old man. I do not want to see that for him. He deserves better."

"That, my lord, is something we at least agree on, but I would ask that you do not trick him in such a way again. It was not becoming of you."

The marquess seemed suitably chastised. "I promise I shall not. But what of you and your concern for him? I did not think you even liked Athelby."

What the marquess said was certainly true. They were not close, nor was she very fond of him up until the night she found him vomiting onto roses. But she had been associated with his family as a young girl and owed it to his grandmother to look out for him if she had to. "My love for his grandmother and our friendship as children make me say these things. Do not read anything further into that concern, my lord."

The dance took them from each other for a few steps

before they were reunited. "Well, you may not be attentive toward the duke, but he's certainly taking notice of you," the marquess said. "Even now, he's watching, probably trying to find fault with both our steps."

Darcy frowned. It was not very becoming of his lordship to laugh at his friend so. Having had enough of him, she stepped out of his hold and dipped a quick curtsy. "If you'll excuse me. I find I do not wish to dance with you, my lord."

He raised his brows, clearly shocked. "You do not?"

"No," she said. "I think you're a dolt."

The few people about them gasped and some of the gentlemen laughed before she walked over to the duke and took his hand, pulling him onto the dance floor. "Shall we?" she asked.

With elegance and ease, Athelby guided her back into the steps. They were silent for a time before he said, "You seem displeased. Is anything the matter?"

"Only that you have very strange friends, Your Grace. If I were you, I would watch what you say around the marquess. He does not seem true to me."

"If what has your feathers ruffled is solely due on my behalf—for my honor—do not tax yourself. Aaron is just as honest as I am, if not a little less cutting. If he teased me before you, and said something that seems beneath our friendship, you should not worry about it. For I shall not."

"He said that you have a concern in me, beyond that of a friend."

The duke looked down at her, and she was shocked to recognize desire in his grey orbs. Who would've thought the too-proper duke even had such emotions in his indifferent body and mind?

"He is mistaken."

Really... Darcy narrowed her eyes, not believing that for a moment. "I'm relieved to hear it."

ATHELBY COULD SEE by the disbelieving lift of Darcy's brows that she did not agree with his statement, and she would be right. After her help the other evening, and the lack of rumors concerning his embarrassing slip of etiquette, she'd proven to him that she was trustworthy. More so probably than his oldest friend Lord Aaron.

"Do you know that there are two bets on me at White's as to who I'll take as a lover or even a husband?"

He pulled her closer than he ought, blaming it on the crush of dancers around them. "I do, and I have stated to those who have placed a bet that they are vulgar and not gentlemanly in the least."

She smiled up at him, and the breath in his lungs seized. Blast it, she was so beautiful, so kissable, that it hurt to deny himself. But she was not for him. The de Merles were too wild, non-manageable, and certainly did not play by the rules by which he set his life.

But to taste her, if only once, would surely sate him for the rest of his days.

"How do you know of this bet in any case?"

This time she laughed, a rich, intoxicating sound that almost undid his years of strict decorum and made him seize her here and now. Kiss those smiling lips until they were both lost to each other and noted nothing and no one else around them. He ripped his gaze from hers and stared steadfastly over her shoulder. Anywhere but at the temptation that was in his arms, which would lead him to ruination just like his brother.

"I know everything that happens in your secret little

White's, and I may have at first been a little put out about the bet, but I now find it quite amusing."

He couldn't see anything remotely comical about the bet. It was belittling to her and to anyone who partook in such scandalous behavior. Darcy did not deserve to be the butt of jokes and games of his fellow man. "I do not."

"I can tell by your face that you do not. But should I play the little game that all the gentlemen at White's are betting on? Who would you suggest that I marry? Or, alternatively, who should I make my lover?"

He stuttered, unable to respond straight away. "I wouldn't know how to give such advice."

She harrumphed, and he refused to look at her. How could he when he didn't want her thinking of any of the gentlemen of the ton in that way? Not that she was for him either, he reminded himself. He simply thought it best for Darcy to remain a spinster for the remainder of her days. Perhaps travel the continent and become an expert in embroidery. Anything but to marry again where he would have to watch her from afar.

"So you're not able to tell me which men I should consider and those I should keep well away from? You're around the gentlemen when they're ensconced in their little club. I should think you'd hear everything they really think and mean, certainly more than any woman would ever know."

"Even if I did know of a few gentlemen who'd be suitable, I could not in good conscience tell you of such things. It's against my moral judgement." He lost contact with her for a few steps before he pulled her out of the dance to stand beside a partially open window.

"Tell me, Your Grace, do you think your high moral judgement will keep you warm in bed? Do you not yearn for the comfort of a woman, to have her love you in all ways that a man and woman should?"

Athelby swallowed. This conversation was well beyond his knowledge. He tugged at his cravat that was suddenly too tight. "You should not say such things."

Darcy moved closer than she ought now that they were no longer dancing and yet, to his dismay and pleasure, he did not pull back or move away to where he was safe. Damn it, he was turning into his brother. A man who could not say no to a woman.

"Would you, do you think Your Grace, be suitable as my lover?"

He turned and looked at her, and blast, he could not hide what he'd tried to for so many months. To tell her that she was all that he thought of when alone. That when she'd been married to that coxcomb the Earl of Terrance, the thought of her with him in his bed, lying with him night after night, had tormented him. The stoic, cold man that he was could not wholly be blamed on his reckless sibling. A lot had to do with his jealousy of the earl and who he had as his wife.

But as much as he longed to have Darcy, he would never succumb to the baser elements that haunted many fellow men, not just him. He was not a rake, a rogue who would have any woman he wished, only to discard her when he no longer had use for her. Or engage in stupid carriage races where you ended up dead.

The woman he married would be an upstanding, well-connected virgin. A woman of impeccable manners. Not the bedevilling minx staring up at him right at this moment, daring him with her crystal blue eyes to bend down and kiss her before all the ton.

"Never, Lady de Merle. We would not suit." His words were cutting, and he tore his attention away to the gathered throng so as to ignore the flash of hurt and despair that had entered her eyes.

"What about your friend the Marquess of Aaron? Maybe I should take him to my bed."

He clasped her arm, pulling her to look at him. "You will not, and nor will he."

She raised one brow in disbelief. "And you know this how?"

"Because I told him to keep his filthy hands off you." He turned on his heel and strode toward the supper room doors just as a footman announced the short repast was ready. He did not turn back, yet the burn of Darcy's gaze at his back scolded him and did not abate for the remainder of the evening.

***

Darcy found it hard to sleep that night, and many nights after, for thinking about what the Duke of Athelby had said to her before he scuttled off like an injured wolf.

It wasn't to be borne. He could not just say something like that and then leave! And no matter how much they might dislike one another, there was an odd attraction between them that they both needed to admit to.

Act on…

She lay back in her bath, splashing water onto the floor. *What am I to do with this absurd attraction?* Athelby was not the kind of man who indulged in liaisons. Something tugged inside of her. Had he ever been with a woman at all, in any way? Not just intimately, but even a simple kiss?

After what he'd told her of his brother, she doubted he would've allowed himself the slightest slip in giving into the base desires of man.

Tonight was the Foxes' masquerade ball, a sought-after event that marked the middle of the season. She had not attended when married since Terrance had forbidden it.

Of course, his denying of her own entertainments did not stop him from taking part, and often returning home with ripped clothing, a missing mask, and numerous love bites over his neck and body.

The door to her room opened then closed just as quickly before the light footsteps of her maid pattered across the Aubusson rug. "Your gown is ready, my lady. Would you like me to help you out of the bath?"

"Yes, thank you," Darcy said, standing, and took her maid's hand as she stepped out. The gown of royal blue with a second skirt of embroidered gold thread would suit her dark colouring and golden mask. "I'll wear my hair half down this evening, Jane."

"Yes, my lady."

Within a couple of hours, Darcy found herself in the ballroom for the masked ball. The terrace doors were open, allowing the hundreds of revellers to walk the lawns and gain some air should they wish it.

The abundance of candles, the patterned gowns, and the beautiful masks would make finding anyone she knew difficult, and yet there was only one person that she really wanted to find.

She danced a couple of reels and the first waltz with a gentleman who played as coy and secretive as she did. For her first masquerade, she found she was enjoying it very much. To be incognito was liberating, and she was pleased to find her flirting abilities had not died along with her husband.

It was while dancing a jig, where many a partner was changed during the movement of the dance, that a shiver of awareness ran down her spine. Her new partner clasped her hands and moved her along with the dance.

She looked up and recognised Athelby's grin. "We meet again, Your Grace."

"I see my mask has not fooled you." He did not sound pleased, but Darcy paid no heed to his tone. Tonight, she would kiss this man if it were the last thing she did. Once and for all, she would see if this absurd attraction she had to him was warranted or some figment of her warped imagination.

"I would know you anywhere, Athelby." And if she did not recognize him by sight, her body alerted her to his presence. Just as it had this evening, and if she were honest, for many years before.

ATHELBY FROWNED DOWN AT DARCY. Anything but let the little minx know that having her in his arms again left him reeling, warring with his morals on what he desired to do and what he ought to do.

The biggest conundrum he had, and one he hated to admit to, was that Darcy made him nervous. Each and every time he was around her he fought not to babble like a fool. And after their discussion about who would suit her best as a lover or future husband, something told him that his nervousness would only increase.

"I find that hard to believe, Lady de Merle." He used her title, not her given name. The less intimacy between them the better. Or so he told himself. Even though the dance commanded he change partners, he kept her in his arms.

"Do you? I simply have to look for the angriest-looking gentleman, the one who's scowling at everyone, and I know I've found you. Even behind your mask you ooze annoyance. You're like an elephant trying to hide behind a stick."

"Really, what an absurd analogy." Athelby tried to take offence, and yet he found his lips twitching to smile. He would again discuss this maddening attraction to a woman who wasn't suitable to be his duchess at his next visit to Dr. Duncan. Surely there was a pill of sorts one could take to cure themselves of feelings.

The dance ended, and he walked her toward the terrace doors. "Would you care for a stroll? You seem a little flushed."

"As long as you do not try to seduce me, Duke." Darcy grinned up at him and slid her arm about his, leading him outdoors. The air was chill, but refreshing after the stifling ballroom.

"Your reputation is safe with me. I should say, you're probably the safest woman in England right about now." Not exactly true... Out of the corner of his eye, he watched her looking up at the stars, and his gut clenched at how very pretty she was, the mask no impediment to her beauty.

They strolled toward the back of the garden, the sound of running water and some whispered voices all that could be heard. With the Foxes' estate backing onto Hyde Park, the gardens were quite extensive, and there were many places people could disappear to for a tryst or stroll.

Athelby would not be one of them.

A marble bench glowed under the moonlight, and he led Darcy toward it to sit for a time. Taking the opportunity, he pulled off his mask, and was glad to see Darcy did the same.

"Have you ever kissed a woman, Your Grace?"

The question caught him by surprise and he spluttered before answering, "Of course." He'd kissed his grandmother hello and goodbye, and other family members too. So, in all truth, what he stated was not a lie. Not really. But he understood her question, and the truth was, no. He'd never kissed a woman with passion. To make them both yearn for and crave what kisses were wont to lead to. His brother kissed too many women in his younger years, and his foolish actions all in the name of women led to his early demise. He would not make the same mistake. He was the last surviving Athelby heir. If he died, the ducal title would die with him.

He could feel Darcy regarding him, and as much as he wanted to not look at her, he couldn't help himself. He turned, and the pit of his stomach clenched in the most intoxicating way. A feeling he'd never suffered before, but wanted to again and again.

"Would you like to kiss me, Athelby?"

God damn it yes, he did. "No."

CHAPTER 4

Damn him to Hades and back. After such a question, the last thing Darcy thought any sane man would do was stand upright as if he'd been poked by a scalding fire iron and take ten paces. She remained on the seat, watching him, not yet ready to give up her quest for the evening.

Athelby needed to be kissed, to be shown that just because his brother may have passed away after a very reckless life, it did not mean that one kiss with her would lead him down the same road. The man needed to be shown that life could be passionate without peril, disaster, and death. Not everyone was like his late sibling.

"No, I would not. I do not know what game you're playing, my lady, but I do not find it amusing in the least."

She shrugged. "I want to kiss you, so I asked if the feeling was reciprocated. You have stated it is not. There are no hurt feelings or broken hearts, I merely wanted to show you that by kissing me, the ducal line shall not fall. It'll be there tomorrow just as it is today. That is all."

"You wanted to use me?"

She barked out a laugh, not the most ladylike thing to do, and yet for the first time ever, his grace didn't scold her about it. "No, I wanted to kiss you. Simply a man and a woman enjoying each other." She stood and sauntered over to him, amused when he retreated away from her until his back came up against a large oak tree.

"I do not want to kiss you, Lady de Merle."

"No? Well, that is a shame." She ran her hand down the lapels of his coat, the accelerated breathing and heart rate telling her more about what the duke was feeling than what he was saying. "Aren't you the least bit curious about what it would be like? We've rarely got along, but maybe we would get along grandly in this regard."

The more she spoke about kissing the man, the more she wanted to reach up and do it. Take his lips, that looked perfectly in proportion to the rest of his face, and see if they were as soft as she suspected they were.

"We would not," he said, his attention snapping to her mouth.

Darcy bit her bottom lip, and didn't miss the clench of his jaw. Oh yes, the duke wanted to kiss her. And if she were a woman of the world, which she was in a way, he wanted to do it with a desperation that she herself admitted.

"Just a little one. You wouldn't deny a lady that small request, would you?"

He frowned, and she clasped the lapels of his jacket, going up on her toes so as to reach him better. "Do not deny me, Duke," she whispered.

"Damn you, Darcy."

She gasped as the little control she'd had just a moment ago vanished and she was seized by the duke, wrenched against his chest, his mouth coming down hard against hers, his tongue thrusting against her own.

She moaned, shocked and delighted at the pleasure that coursed through her. She had not anticipated wanting to do a hell of a lot more with the duke than kiss, but she certainly did now.

This would never be enough. She wanted more, so much more, and the hard part would be how she could get what she wanted. How to convince the duke that they could be together like this, without his fear of becoming a debauched rake like his brother impeding his decision.

He held her firm, his hands slipping further around her back where one thumb brushed against her bare shoulders. Darcy tried to keep up, but her mind was spinning. The duke could kiss, very well, considering he'd not kissed anyone like this before.

He may say otherwise, but knowing him and his ways, Darcy was sure she was the first.

Leaning up further on her toes, her breasts brushed him as she slid her hands through his hair, keeping him exactly where she wanted him. The kiss turned molten, and she grappled not to lose the little control she still held.

ATHELBY SLID his hand over her delectable body, barely hidden by her silk gown, and clasped her thigh, lifting it a little against his own. His breath came out in a rush and his heart threatened to burst. Darcy kissed him with a desire that ignited him to flame. His cock hardened, painfully so, and her pleading whimper when she rubbed against him almost made him lose himself in his breeches.

He ought to be ashamed of himself. This was not what he should be doing with her. His moral compass had completely deserted him. He tried to think of his brother —his death and the woman behind it. Remind himself that his sibling's recklessness over a woman—a woman the family would never have allowed him to marry in any case —was the reason he participated in the stupid carriage race that killed him.

But when Darcy slowed the kiss, her tongue coaxing his, all Athelby wanted to do was ravish her. Take everything and all that she would give. Her kiss was all that he thought it would be, and it would never be enough. Not for him.

"Let me court you, my dear. I need more than just this one night," he said, taking her lips again as if his life depended on it.

Darcy's mind whirred at the mention of courting. She'd already married a man who was controlling, mean, and vindictive. Not that the duke was vindictive, but he could certainly be cutting, and he liked control most of all. She might wish to take him as a lover, but never as a husband. She did not escape by chance one terrible marriage, only to enter another of very similar particulars.

She wrenched herself out of his arms, and he stepped toward her, his gaze unfocused and mad with desire. "What are you doing?" he asked, breathless.

"Saving us from a mistake." She righted her gown and fixed her hair, holding up a hand when he reached for her. "No more, Your Grace. I shouldn't have teased you so into kissing me, and I apologize."

He stood there, shock and annoyance settling on his features. Then he took a calming breath and ran a hand through his hair, looking about to see if anyone had been watching their blatant fondling session in the garden.

"It is I who should ask forgiveness. I was carried away with unexpected emotion." He bowed. "Good evening, Lady de Merle."

Darcy placed a hand across her lips to stop herself from asking him to stay, to finish what she'd feared for some weeks now was between them. Desire—a scorching, intoxicating need for each other—that she feared she had sparked to life tonight with her teasing and their kiss.

He collected his mask, and she watched him disappear up the garden path. She sat back down on the bench. There was only one way forward from tonight. She would have to keep well away from the duke, not attend any events that he might also attend, and try to keep herself from doing exactly what she wanted to again.

Take the Duke of Athelby to her bed.

ATHELBY HAD, up to tonight, been successful in avoiding Darcy de Merle. But upon entering the musical loo hosted by Earl Musgrove and his wife, which was to be followed by a light supper repast, his days of avoidance were over.

He stood at the front of the music room, where Lady Musgrove had set up chairs before a makeshift stage where fellow guests would perform, and a small orchestra would play to complement the singers.

In the past, he had enjoyed these types of events very much. He did not have to converse too much with those attending, and with supper served just afterward, most were eating, and therefore conversation was again not overly required.

His location gave him the perfect opportunity to watch others as they arrived. He nodded as the Marquess of Aaron talked to him about the latest Crown Lands Act in Parliament, but his mind was otherwise engaged. In fact, his mind and body had not been his own for the past fortnight. It belonged to another.

Endless hours of reliving the kiss he'd shared with Darcy haunted his mind. His body ached as it never had before. He'd lost count of how many times he'd woken in the middle of the night, his cock as hard as a rock. Sometimes, at his lowest ebb, he'd found his hand had been clasped about it, stroking it, teasing it as he wished she had.

It was utterly mortifying and inappropriate, and he would quite literally die of shame should anyone know what he'd been thinking. What he'd been longing to do with the little minx who stood laughing at something her friend Lady Oliver was saying. The way he was going, he would be as debauched as his brother before the Season's end.

"If you keep staring at de Merle the way you are, you'll be made to marry the chit. What have you done with the lady that's made you so possessed with her person?" Aaron asked, taking a sip of his wine.

Not as much as I'd like to have done.

Damn it. He wrenched his gaze down to the floor and studied the parquetry for a moment. "I've not done anything with her ladyship. She merely annoys me."

Torments me...

"The betting book at White's now states that Lord Thomas and Sir Fraser are front runners in contention as her lovers. They've been quite attentive to her, and she's certainly allowed them to show their affection, if you understand me."

"She's allowed them to kiss her?" He shut his mouth with a snap and stood tall, lifting his chin so as not to show that the mention of Darcy kissing another hurt. Hurt like bloody hell.

"I understand Sir Fraser has had the pleasure, but then, you know with these young bucks, they often tell tales just to boost their own self-importance."

"They should not be associating their scandalous behavior with Lady de Merle if it isn't true. Her reputation could be tarnished by such rumors."

"She is striking, I must admit. And I've meant to apologize for my behavior the other week. My teasing of you was not warranted, and I'm sorry I spoke of you in such a way to Lady de Merle."

Athelby nodded once. "Apology accepted. But you should not concern yourself. I never take any notice of your nonsense when you're in your cups."

The marquess snorted, lifting his wine glass up in salute. "As you should." He paused for a moment. "Lady de Merle does seem to take an interest in you though, Athelby. Are you sure you're telling me the truth that there is nothing between the two of you?"

There was a lot between them, but nothing he would ever admit verbally. Not even to his closest friend. He raised his attention to where he knew Darcy was located and their gazes locked. Again, his stomach somersaulted in the most dizzying, intoxicating way and he clenched his jaw.

Damn it. He'd hoped after being away from her these past weeks such a reaction would not occur. How wrong he'd been. If anything, it was worse.

Denial, it would seem, made the bond grow stronger.

"You've kissed. I can see it between the two of you as clear as air. And you want to do it again. Admit it, man, you've had a tryst with de Merle."

"No tryst, just a kiss." Blast, he had not intended to say a thing about it. He wrenched his attention away from Darcy and frowned at his friend. "Do not tell anyone of what you know, and do not put my name down as a contender for her ladyship's hand, either in marriage or as a lover."

"I think you could be a contender for both, for the way she's looking at you right now, I would say you're more likely to be her lover before anything else."

The thought of having Darcy beneath him in his bed made his blood beat at a crescendo that even the instruments about to play could not reach. "I will not sleep with her. Ever." To do so went against all his morals, the way in which he'd lived his life. Fleeting liaisons were not who he was or ever would be. He was a respectable, upstanding duke. Not a rake.

"Oh well, from the looks of Sir Fraser you've missed your chance. And Lady de Merle seems quite pleased by his attentions, if I'm any judge of character."

"I do not care." Athelby sat and steadfastly refused to move his attention from the stage, even though the singing was yet to commence. Aaron sat beside him, shaking his head, but apparently deciding not to voice whatever it was he was thinking.

Athelby thought that was for the best, considering his mood was decidedly soured. Whether it was due to Darcy fawning over another gentleman, acting inappropriately yet again, or because it was not he himself that she was acting inappropriately with, he couldn't be sure.

THE MUSICAL NIGHT hosted by the Earl and Countess Musgrove was something Darcy had been looking forward to, up until the point when she saw Athelby in all his elegance standing beside the Marquess of Aaron, his dark, intense inspection of her rattling her more than she'd like to admit and leaving her flushed.

She had resolved to keep her distance from him, and had done quite well until now. Their set was wide and varied, and it hadn't been hard to avoid him at the balls and parties they were both invited to. If she heard from his grandmother when he was to attend an event, she simply ensured that she attended at a different time.

It had all worked out splendidly, until this evening. A musical loo was not something she'd thought the duke would be interested in, and yet here he was, as handsome as ever, cold and aloof as he'd always been.

She shook her head as she ate a crab cake during the supper repast. After the music he'd seemed to disappear, and she assumed he'd returned home or moved on to attend another event. The fact that his absence left her a little bored and forlorn was not to be considered. She was determined never to marry again, no matter how enticing being courted by the Duke of Athelby might be. She could not risk another bad marriage like the one she'd had to endure with Terrance.

"Fran, darling, I'm going to use the ladies' retiring room, and then I think I shall leave. I wish to go for a ride tomorrow morning, and I'll never rise should I not head home soon."

Her friend handed her glass to her husband, who was standing with them. "Would you like me to accompany you?"

Darcy waved her suggestion away. "No, I shall be fine, and my maid is waiting for me there. You stay here and enjoy this delicious repast."

She exited through the door she'd seen other ladies slip through. A footman explained where the retiring room was and pointed her in the right direction. She walked past a bank of windows, some of which were bay in design. Red velvet drapes hung down on all of them, allowing privacy to anyone who sat upon the seat overlooking the gardens if they so wished. Walking past one that was drawn closed, she stifled a scream when a large hand came out and pulled her into the secretive alcove.

"You!" The wild, ravenous look on Athelby's face gave her pause, and she didn't say another word.

"Yes, me," he said, pushing her against the wall and taking her lips in a searing kiss. Against her better judgement and rules, her past mistakes and wishes for the future, Darcy clung to him, all but climbed up against his person and made herself as close as she possibly could while the kiss carried on.

It was too much. This need, the all-consuming obsession with him, could not be possible. "Touch me, Cameron," she gasped as he tried to lift her up to get them as close as achievable.

Failing that, he moaned and rocked against her instead. One hand fiddled with the base of her gown, before the cool night air kissed her ankle, calf and then thankfully, finally, her thigh. Athelby paused, pulling back a little to stare at her. "I don't know what to do."

Darcy fought to understand what he was saying through her desire-consumed mind before understanding dawned. Taking his hand, she guided him to where she wanted him to touch her most.

He didn't pull away and stop what she was showing him, and the fact that this man, a duke no less, was not skilled in the ways of what a woman wanted suited her. He was hers to mould. To teach touches, kisses, and whatever else they did together. To know no one else had been with Athelby like this was a powerful elixir that was hard to deny.

At first, his touch was hesitant, too careful, as if he was scared to hurt her. This kind of endless teasing was almost enough to send pleasure ricocheting through her. "Slide your hand against me, explore and learn me, Cameron."

. . .

CAMERON HAD NEVER, ever wanted to take a woman as much as he fought not to take Darcy. She stood before him, his to take, her legs spread as the wall supported her while he teased and touched the most private of parts of a woman.

When he'd pulled her into the curtained space, he'd not thought this would happen. He'd meant to chastise her for teasing Sir Fraser and leading the poor fellow on. But the moment she'd entered the space, all he'd wanted to do was kiss her. Taste her one more time.

The woman's anatomy was not as he'd expected it to be, and touching Darcy like this allowed him to learn what she liked, what made her gasp and cling to him like he was the only other living soul on earth.

"Athelby," she gasped when his finger found a peculiar, small entrance. Seeing if his touching of her there was something she enjoyed, he slid one finger a little way inside.

Darcy kissed him hard, her tongue meshing with his, and emboldened, he slid his finger fully in. It was then he realized she was riding his hand, just as he imagined a woman would ride a man's phallus.

His balls ached and were tighter than he'd ever known them to be. Other than the times he'd woken up in bed, panting and as hard as hell after dreaming of the woman who currently resided in his arms.

"I'm going to come," she whispered against his lips.

Her lips parted, her head tilting back as she continued to ride him. Athelby nibbled and kissed her while she peaked, her bottom lip clasped tight in her teeth to stop any notifying sound. In time she regained her composure, and already he longed to have her in such a state again.

He'd never slept with a woman before, probably a fact that Darcy now knew, and the pleasure she seemed to experience made him yearn to know if it would be the same for him. He'd gained so much enjoyment from watching her, to be more involved, finding his own release... would it be as addictive as he imagined it would be.

Just the thought had him wishing she'd undo his front falls, sit him on the bench at the window, and ride him until they both found release.

Their gazes locked, and instead of pulling away, Darcy wrapped her arms around his shoulders, kissing him lightly before she said words that were never truer. "We have a problem, Athelby."

And they did. A big one.

CHAPTER 5

Darcy sat astride her grey mare, Montclair, and galloped as fast as the horse would carry her down Rotten Row. The park was deserted, bar her groom Peter who sat atop his own horse under a copse of trees not too far away.

The sensation of flying always invigorated Darcy, and she patted her mare as they trotted to a stop, then turned her back toward her groom. They had been out for some time already, and soon the park would have the early morning riders who would not take well the sight of a woman, astride and galloping down the row. All faux pas according to the ton, and rules that Darcy always enjoyed ignoring.

She trotted back to Peter and smiled. "Time to return I think."

"Right ye are, my lady."

Darcy rode ahead, and as they walked the horses across the park toward the northern gate, a group of men entered on beautiful, well-bred mounts that Darcy couldn't help but appreciate. But one man stood out more than the rest.

Athelby.

They stopped and dipped their hats and Darcy in turn smiled but didn't slow. "Good morning, gentlemen," she said, liking the fact that all of them threw her admiring glances. Today she had worn her newly purchased silk jockey bonnet, which went perfectly with her navy-blue riding suit with gold buttons, and she looked almost regimental. Not to mention the colouring always complemented her blue eyes.

The men moved on—all but one.

"Go ahead, Peter," she said, stopping now that Athelby had. "I wish to have a word with the duke."

"Yes, my lady," he said, doing as she bid.

Athelby turned his horse to come up alongside hers. Darcy raised one brow but didn't say a word. After they had left each other two nights past, she'd not seen him at any events. Was he avoiding her again? More than likely, and it wasn't to be borne. He could not raise such deliciousness within her and then disappear. Her husband had never given her such pleasure in the short amount of time they were married, and other than giving herself release a few small times, with Athelby it was the first time a man had raised such emotions.

She wouldn't allow it. The Duke of Athelby was going to be her lover if it were the last thing she did this Season.

"Are you well, my lady?" he asked, his tone distant, and yet his eyes were the window to his soul, and she could see he was struggling. What that struggle was exactly, she couldn't be sure. Wanting her while fighting the emotion, or her ineligibility due to his standards, she would assume. He'd always been such a stickler for rules, so to disregard them after finding pleasure in her arms would go against all that he believed in.

He wanted her, of that she had no doubt. But would he

act on it, really act on it, and make her fully his? That, she wasn't certain of.

"I am very well, thank you. And you?" If he was going to be all formal and absurd, then so was she.

"I am well." His jaw clenched, and he looked away, adjusting his seat a little. The action made her attention snap to his thighs, and she bit her bottom lip seeing that he had very muscular legs and that the tan breeches he had on were very much accentuating his fine form.

It was crass of her to ogle the man in such a way, but really, what was one to do when she found him absurdly attractive, and if she had her way, she'd help him out of those breeches and not let him get back into them again until she was fully satisfied?

"I want to kiss you." His words sounded torn, a deep rumble that tumbled her common sense into dangerous ground.

Ignoring all sense of decorum, and considering they were a little way from the gates of Hyde Park, Darcy tempted fate. She leaned toward the duke and caught his gaze. "Then kiss me, Athelby."

His attention slid to her lips and for a moment she actually believed he would do as she asked, before he thought better of it and straightened his spine. "I cannot kiss you here."

She shrugged, knowing that was too true, but wanting to tease him a little about it in any case. "Pity, for I so dearly would love you to." Darcy pulled her horse to come around the back of his and took the opportunity to slide one finger across his bottom and down one leg as she went. "Are you attending the Leeders' ball this evening?"

"Yes," he said, pushing her hand off his thigh.

She grinned. "Maybe we can continue to further our acquaintance there?" Her words finally and triumphantly brought out a small grin from the duke, and Darcy chuckled. How handsome and approachable he was when he wasn't scowling at everyone, growling like a lion with a prickle in its paw.

"Well then," she said, moving off. "I shall see you there, Your Grace." She trotted away and didn't turn back to look at the duke, but she knew he would be watching her, more than likely debating all the pros and cons of doing what they both wanted.

Each other.

BY MIDNIGHT, Darcy had all but given up hope that the duke would attend the Leeders' annual ball. She stood beside a grouping of house plants and swallowed down the last of the numerous glasses of champagne she'd already had this evening.

Damn him. If he thought to avoid her again, run away like a little man-child, he could think again. She wouldn't allow it. Even though tonight there was little she could do.

This late in the evening, the guests were well in their cups, and the dancing was still the focal point, although some of the gentlemen had wandered into the card room and commenced gambling.

Darcy sighed and placed her glass on a passing footman's tray, and debated taking another or going home. Even her friend Fran had left some hours ago, and Darcy had only stayed due to the possibility Athelby would arrive.

He would pay for this deception.

She took another glass and sipped. She would give him until the end of this drink to arrive and then she was going home. Distracted by her annoyance at the duke, she didn't notice the gentleman who came to stand beside her until a warm finger touched the nape of her neck and slid down the full length of her spine, all the way down to her bottom.

Darcy grinned as hope bloomed in her chest. She took another sip. "How very inappropriate of you, Duke."

He leaned close to her ear, his whispered words igniting fire in her blood. "I want to be inappropriate with you. Only you."

The breath in her lungs seized and she swallowed. She wasn't used to the duke turning the tables on her and being the one to seduce. It was normally she who goaded and taunted. Even so, it was refreshing and so very arousing to have him do it instead.

"Dance with me, Darcy."

This time she did place her glass down on a passing footman's tray, and let the duke lead her onto the dance floor for a waltz. She went into his arms willingly, needing to be close to him, to smell his freshly laundered clothes, his sandalwood cologne, and something else that was just Athelby.

A little alarm went off in her mind that she was getting herself too involved with him, seeing possibility where no possibility should be seen. "You're a very good dancer for a man who doesn't often take to the floor."

He moved them with grace and ease about the room. Considering his height and her own, they fit perfectly, and their dance was effortless.

"I had a very good teacher, and of course I was the most avid student."

"Why is that so easy to believe?" Darcy chuckled, and he frowned.

"You should not mock people merely because they take an interest in all that they learn. I have never done things by halves and I should not start now."

"And yet," she said, wanting to harass him a little more,

"you've teased me, only completed half of what I want you to do with me, so who is the bad student now?"

Desire burned in his gaze and she shuffled closer still. "I want you in my bed, Athelby. And I want it soon."

He tripped a little, but righted them quickly enough that no other dancers about them noticed. "Lady de Merle, while I—"

"Don't you dare, Your Grace. You will finish what we both started. What we both want."

For a time he was silent, and Darcy fought not to lose her temper with him. It was not at all gentlemanly, if this was a gentlemanly act at all, to cry off and leave her wanting him fiercely, while he pushed down his own desires and refused her. Right at this moment, she damned his brother to the pits of hell for scaring his younger sibling into being a prude.

"Darcy, I..." Again, he stumbled over his words, and she took pity on him. Maybe he wasn't going to cry off. Run away like she thought he would.

"What, Athelby? What say you?"

The little frown line was back between his brows, and she wanted to reach up and smooth it away with her finger. But here and now was not the time.

"I'm...I'm... God damn it all to hell," he swore. "I've never been with a woman in that way before," he whispered, looking about to ensure no one was listening.

Darcy didn't react, for she knew that already. Had suspected when he'd not known how to touch her. The kissing he had taken to very well and quickly indeed, but the touching of her at the musical loo had only occurred because she'd told him what to do, where to touch.

To know no one had had the man in her arms before was more exciting than anything she'd ever known in her life. To have it confirmed was doubly so. Maybe that was why husbands found gaining brides who were untouched so arousing. She could certainly agree with the notion a lot more now that she had Athelby in much the same way.

"I know," she said, playing with the little bit of hair at the base of his neck. "And if anything, knowing this only makes me want you all the more."

Their dance had slowed and they stood scandalously close, but for the first time ever, it seemed the Duke of Athelby was not concerned with proper etiquette and correct behavior.

"I will not have you at a ball," he whispered, pulling her into a tight spin as they came to the end of the room. "I want you in my bed. Not in a window alcove."

"I found our last rendezvous in the window alcove very rewarding indeed. I could make the same a possibility for you. There are ways, you know, for a woman to pleasure a man in much the same way."

He sucked in a breath and closed his eyes for a moment. "The thought of us, of you doing such things to me…please do not say it here. No one wants to see the Duke of Athelby hobbling off the dance floor with his cock pushing out the front of his breeches."

Darcy laughed, taking a quick glance downwards just for fun. "Take me back to your home. Let me show you all that there can be between a man and a woman."

"No. I do not wish to rush this with you."

Although disappointed, she could understand his caution. "Very well, we shall take it slow. But promise me that after this dance we will leave, together and in your carriage. If I do not kiss you soon, I shall expire."

Thankfully the dance came to an end, and they were able to make their goodbyes to their hosts for the evening. Darcy called for her carriage and spoke to her maid, notifying her that she had other transport to return home.

Using the shield of her own carriage, she walked two steps and jumped up into the duke's. No sooner had she sat on the squabs than did the horses move on and they were on their way.

"I told the coachman to drive around until advised otherwise."

Darcy went about untying the rolled-up blinds and pulling them down over the windows.

"What are you doing?" he asked, not moving from the seat opposite her, simply watching her with amusement.

"Making this little abode private so no one can see in."

"In that case…" Leaning forward, he snipped the locks on the doors and now they were fully alone and unable to be disturbed.

Settling back on her seat, Darcy watched him for a moment.

"What now, de Merle?" he asked, grinning a little.

She bit her lip, desire curling throughout her body. "What indeed, Athelby."

LATER THAT EVENING Athelby would wonder how the hell he'd not known a carriage could be a vessel of pure, unadulterated pleasure. For years he'd travelled within such an abode, seen couples alight from their vehicles and often deliberated why the women looked starry-eyed and the men most pleased.

His brother had certainly looked that way often enough.

Now he knew the reasons behind all that. For Darcy de Merle had shown him what they could have between them if he chose.

Darcy moved from the other seat and came to sit beside him. Hell's blood, she smelt good enough to eat. As sweet as a rose and just as pretty. Unable to deny himself, he cupped her jaw and kissed the side of her mouth. Small little kisses across her neck toward the base of her ear. His attempt to seduce her seemed to work, if her soft sighs were any indication.

"I'm going to pleasure you, Duke. Now sit back," she said, pushing him against the squabs. "And enjoy."

Damn it, he bit back a groan at her lascivious promise. As it was his cock sat rigid in his pants, ready and waiting for her to do whatever it was she had planned.

"Promise me that whatever I do, you'll not try to stop me. Know that what I'm doing is because I want to, that it's acceptable and will be enjoyable."

"Very well," he said, not willing to deny her anything.

He shifted his legs further apart as slowly, delicately she undid his front falls. He tried not to cringe when his cock sprang forward, eager for her touch. She ran her finger along the top of his cock, taking the little bead of moisture that sat there and sliding it between her lips, licking it.

"Fuck," he gasped, having never used such a word or imagined such an action was possible, or that anyone would want to do such a thing for that matter. But seeing Darcy do so had his heart beating a million times too fast, his body not his own. For right now, at this very moment, Darcy owned him. All of him.

And damn it all to hell, he wanted to do the same to her. Lie her back on the squabs, part her lovely long legs and lick her from ankle to core. The thought of what she'd taste like there, the crude naughtiness of it, left his cock more rigid and he fought not to clasp Darcy's cheeks and guide her over him.

Kneeling in front of him, her gaze captured his and her perfect pink tongue came out and licked him from base to tip. He fought not to pass out from the wonderful sensation of having her lick his cock.

He'd missed out on so much, and the thought maddened him before she stroked her tongue over his throbbing length again and he lost all thought.

"You're teasing me," he said breathlessly.

She grinned, licking him a third time. "Good things come to those who wait." But she didn't make him wait too much longer. Fascinated, he watched her lips circle the top of his cock and slide down, taking a good third of his phallus before she started the opposite way. He did clasp her face then, if only to anchor himself to reality. Darcy's sucking, licking, teasing of him was relentless, an endless torture that made his stomach clench and his balls ache. Her tongue was soft against his skin, pushing against his pulsating veins.

Dear heaven, he was lost...

For what was probably only minutes, but felt like hours of pleasure, she sucked him, used her small hand about the base of his cock and stroked while her mouth entwined magic about his soul.

Never did he ever have any idea such a thing was possible. That a woman would take a man so, and seemingly enjoy it, if Darcy's aroused moans and breathy sighs were any indication.

The carriage turned a corner and he caught her arm and braced them both by pushing against the window. Darcy adjusted and took him deeper, clasping his balls after each glide of her hand and mouth. The action, a little different than before but more determined, had stars form before his eyes.

He found himself pushing into her mouth—such an ungentlemanly thing to do, but he could not help himself. The need to reach the pinnacle that he'd long denied himself was too much to ignore. He wanted to fuck her mouth, hard, do base things with her and make her come against his own face.

All these thoughts bombarded his mind, and crying out, he climaxed. He tried to pull away, to save some dignity for himself, and her too, but Darcy wouldn't have it. She stayed fixed upon his cock, licking him, sucking and swallowing all that she pulled forth from his release.

His breath ragged, he stared at her as with a little wipe of the corner of her mouth, she sat back on her haunches and grinned. "How do you feel, Your Grace?"

How did he feel? By God, he felt lethargic, hungry for more, intoxicated, drunk on her and what she did to him. "I did not know that it could... That a woman could do such an act to a man. I never listened to the bawdy talk that sometimes occurs at my club."

She came to sit beside him, kissing him gently, slowly, in a way that only aroused him to want more of her. He could taste himself on her, and his cock twitched. "There are lots of things we can do, if you're willing."

He warred with himself. He wanted her, knew that he'd go mad if he didn't have her soon, but to engage in a liaison wasn't something he considered respectable. Darcy needed to be his wife, and perhaps, should he play by her rules for a time, she would come to see the same. He could not just sleep with a woman and then leave her to the wolves, something his brother often did.

He tapped on the roof, signalling the driver to return Darcy home. "Will I see you at the Duncannons' ball two nights from now? I will give you my answer then."

Darcy righted her gown and sat back against the squabs, tidying her hair and ensuring it was similar to how she'd had it set before going out for the night. "Very well, I shall wait to hear what you choose."

"Thank you," he said, frowning at the fact she was annoyed by his hesitation in having an affair with her. Not that he didn't want her—he did. Desperately so.

But by having her, losing himself to her, did that mean he also lost who he was, what he believed to be right? At this time, he couldn't see any other way forward but that path, and he wasn't sure anything, even Darcy, was worth losing his values over.

CHAPTER 6

Darcy sat alone under a large oak at her friend Fran's garden party and covertly watched the Duke of Athelby. He hadn't noticed that she was present, as her chair sat in a lovely shady spot, with some of the branches of the tree hanging down and partially hiding her from view.

She shifted her attention to her friend Fran, and for the first time she noticed a small bump in her friend's otherwise small waistline. She narrowed her eyes on the little mound. When was Fran going to tell her about that little bundle? She smiled at the thought of her best friend not only marrying for love, but starting a family, something she'd wanted to do ever since they were at Mrs. Dew's Finishing School for Young Ladies.

Today the duke wore tan breeches and knee-high boots that were so polished one was sure to see their reflection in them. His bottle-green coat hugged him like a second skin, and she flushed, remembering how she'd managed to delve beneath those fine clothes and give him pleasure. Have his large hands entwine in her hair, pulling her, holding her against his member as she pleasured him. Make the demanding, righteous Duke of Athelby crumble and come apart in her arms. And how delicious it was having him react so.

She crossed her legs, squeezing her thighs a little in expectation. Should they get an opportunity today she would steal him away, lock him up in a room somewhere in the sprawling mansion behind them and have her way with him.

Maybe even make love to him this time. If he wished it.

A footman came by and offered her ices and she took one gratefully. After her less than garden party thoughts, she needed to cool off a little.

The duke continued to stroll through the guests, talking to those who were game enough to speak to the fierce-looking man, before he stopped and quite obviously searched the party. Was he looking for her, maybe?

When their gazes locked, his shoulders slumped just a little. Whether it was in relief at seeing her present, Darcy wasn't sure, but his determined steps toward her certainly implied he'd captured his quarry.

He came to stand at the end of her chair, towering over her, and oh, how she wished he could crawl up the seat to lie atop her, lift her gown and settle between her thighs and take her.

She swallowed, again shifting on her seat as the thought of having him left her needy, a greedy little minx desperate for his touch.

He looked about, not that anyone was nearby. She was the only one lying on the chairs put under the tree to shade guests who wanted to rest for a time. She raised her brow, but didn't say a word, and neither did he. He simply stared at her, his gaze raking her body and leaving her shivering from the raw need that shimmered in his eyes.

His jaw clamped, and he frowned. "Where can we go?"

Oh my… His words made her gasp a little and her heart skip a beat. "Do you wish to be alone, Your Grace?" she asked, playing coy and not simply saying, "me too" as she so wished to.

"I've thought of nothing else but what you did to me the other evening, and it's past time that I returned the favour. It is only right as a gentleman that I do."

"Of course. And as a man who believes manners are a pinnacle we all must strive toward, I would think less of you should you not have offered," Darcy said, coming to stand toe to toe with the duke, "to taste me with your mouth as I tasted you. Enjoyed you, Your Grace." She ran her finger across his bottom lip.

His nose flared as he seemed to struggle with his emotions. Seeing the duke mad for her left her longing for him again. It was the most intoxicating thing she'd ever seen, and her heart did a little flip of rejoicing.

"Somewhere close by. The house is too far away."

Darcy chuckled. The house wasn't all that far, although they would have to cross the lawns and weave their way through the multitude of guests who congregated there, only too ready to stop a duke and try to catch his eye for their daughters.

"There is a summer house hidden in the gardens. If you follow the path until it comes to an end and turn left, you'll see it a little way along. It overlooks the park beyond and the small lake this estate has itself."

"Perfect." The duke strode off in the direction she stated.

Amused, Darcy watched him, then went to talk to a nearby group of women before she too strolled to where they would meet.

Trepidation and expectation made her heart thump

and her stomach clench in excitement. Would the duke enjoy touching a woman so, kissing her in the most intimate of places? Her husband had only ever performed it on her once, and upon awakening the next morning, he'd proceeded to tell her he'd been so far into his cups that he'd thought her one of his mistresses, and that he regretted the action. That he would never do such a thing again.

Before Terrance said that, Darcy had thought that perhaps their marriage could work, that he did find her attractive and wished to only be with her. How wrong she'd been. Such an immature, green fool.

She raised her chin and determinedly continued toward the summer house. The duke was not her deceased spouse. He was a man who desired her, wanted to do all that she wished to do with him. Was passionate and eager to please her, in a sexual regard at least, which was more than her husband had ever been.

She pushed open a small gate on the path, and going through it stopped to admire the summer house. It was a rectangular stone structure, with two large windows and steps leading up to a double glass door. For decoration, the roof had a small castle-style balustrade running about its edges. Darcy had always loved this building, and during the time her friend Fran was being courted by the viscount, they had often spent afternoons here, swimming and enjoying each other's company, while her friend fell further and further in love.

It had been the best of times, and now, hopefully, she would make more delightful memories.

The duke stood in the doorway of their abode, his cravat, coat, and waistcoat nowhere to be seen. Lounging against the wood, he looked casual and so delectably handsome that heat pooled between her legs.

How she wanted him, all of him.

"Waiting for someone, Your Grace?"

He laughed a deep rumble that echoed with determination and need. Shivers slid down her spine and she rushed toward him, eager to have him kiss her, touch her, be with her in any way he was willing.

The moment they touched, a spark lit a flame within her and she kissed him deep and long. The duke did not hold back and, only too willing, met each stroke of her tongue, each clasp of her wandering hands, with that of his own.

Her hair tumbled down about her shoulders as his fingers spiked through it. She pulled his shirt from his breeches and ripped it over his head, leaving his heaving, muscular chest hers to admire.

She stood back a little and admired the view, running her finger over each ripple of muscle. His skin was sun-kissed, making her wonder what he did that he was able to have such a skin tone. The thought of him working shirtless left her mouth dry.

Instead of asking, not wanting to delay what she longed for him to do to her, she leaned forward and kissed where his heart beat fast. Her hands went about his back as she kissed her way up his neck and found his more than willing mouth.

This time the kiss was slow, languorous, an unhurried seduction that made her ache to have him.

"I want you, Athelby." Her voice was breathless and full of need, but she did not care that he would hear that. She could no longer pretend that their little liaison was merely that, a temporary fling. For it was not, not for her at least. Not anymore.

He picked her up, kicking the door closed, and carried her over to a day bed in the middle of the room. For a moment she hoped that he would strip himself of his breeches, but instead, watching her, he slid her dress up over her legs to pool about her waist. Warm air fragranced with roses kissed her skin and she bit her lip as he placed large hands on each of her knees and slowly spread them apart.

Oh, dear lord…

His fingers played with the silk stockings still tied against her thighs before his lips skimmed their way up toward her aching mons. For a man that had never done such a thing before, he certainly seemed to know what he was about.

"You're so beautiful, Darcy." He paused, placing a small kiss to her very core and making her gasp. "Tell me if I'm not doing this right, or you want more or less of what I do."

She could only nod, and watch entranced as he lowered his head again, and this time, slid his tongue against her sex. She moaned, clasping his head lightly and lying back on the cushions to enjoy his wicked, delightful lips.

His touch was unsure at first, tentative, and yet with that, it only made her more frantic. The need coursing through her grew, ebbed and slowed with each of his kisses, each slide of his tongue, until she could not hold back her need any longer.

"Cameron," she gasped. "Touch me with your fingers as well as your mouth. Please," she moaned as he flicked the little nubbin that gave her pleasure with expert authority.

"Like this?" he asked, his words muffled slightly.

She sighed as he slid one finger into her heat, his tongue flicking her toward madness. It was too much and not enough. Unable to help herself, she clutched him between her thighs and rode his mouth as he brought her to climax.

She shouted his name as wave upon wave coursed through her body. The pleasure left her lethargic and sated, and she lay there spent for a moment as he came to lie beside her, pulling her into the crook of his arm.

"I fear I shall never grow tired of having you in such a way, Darcy."

She looked across at him, running her hand over his stubbled jaw. "I fear that I shall never grow tired of you having me in such a way either."

He came to lie on her and kissed her long and slow, her heart doing a silly little flip, one that could only mean one thing. That not only did Darcy de Merle care for the man in her arms, but that she'd possibly grown to love the complicated, opinionated Duke of Athelby.

CHAPTER 7

There was only one explanation for the emotion that was coursing through Athelby's veins right at this moment. Jealousy.

The woman who had pushed his morals to one side and conquered him was waltzing about the floor, more than happy by the looks of her smile and sparkling eyes to be swung about by the blasted Sir Fraser again. Athelby never thought he would have such a reaction to seeing Darcy dancing with another, but now, after all they'd shared these past weeks, she wasn't meant for anyone else. She was his, and he was hers.

He clenched his jaw. A proposal was all that was required of him. Not a small task considering as much as he longed for her, thought of nothing but the minx and enjoyed her company, she was not the most suitable of women to be his duchess.

Darcy de Merle was almost as opinionated as himself. She was a widow and not a woman who allowed anyone to take advantage—certainly not a husband. When she'd married the Earl of Terrance there may have been a time she was green, vulnerable, and eager to please, but not anymore. Now Darcy was hard, wearing her armor like a shell that protected her from harm, and be-damned to anyone who tried to tell her what to do or how to think.

Athelby admired her for it, but when she became his wife, she would have to concede to the rules of his household and society in general. There were expectations and standards that she would need to meet, which he hoped would not be long in coming to fruition.

He just needed to get her to say yes.

The dance was exceedingly long, and by the time Darcy was deposited back with her friend Lady Oliver, Athelby's disposition had gone from cool to glacier.

Darcy took a flute of champagne and commenced an animated discussion over something or other. She was utterly beautiful when enthusiastic in such a way, and he could only hope he could make her as happy once married.

Another gentleman he wasn't familiar with bowed before her and soon she was dancing a reel. Was she ignoring his presence? He'd certainly not been able to catch her eye this past hour. What was she about not looking at him, or even noting his presence, just as he had noted hers upon arrival?

His annoyance spiked and he left the ballroom, heading toward the card room instead. At least there he would not have to watch her flirting, see her happiness when in another man's arms.

The thought brought him up short. Why did he care so much as to what she did with the other gentlemen? They were not engaged, had no understanding. As a widow, Darcy was free to do whatever she wished as long as it was done with discretion.

He slumped into a chair, not heeding who he was

seated across from, and joined in on a game of chance. That he was even in this room, a gambling den where gentlemen threw their living away without a care, was telling indeed. He was not himself, had not been thinking clearly for some weeks now, and it was all due to the little dark-haired minx waltzing about in the ballroom.

Never did he gamble, or drink, and yet tonight he'd found himself doing both. Wilfully ignoring his morals, all because Darcy was not paying any attention to him. He was, in one word, pathetic.

He played several rounds before quitting the game, down a tidy sum due to his distraction. He poured himself a tumbler of whisky, left the room, and wandered the deserted corridors just beyond before finding a billiards room.

The cold, dark, empty space suited his disposition well.

The door shut behind him and he heard the lock snip. Spinning about, he glared at Darcy as she walked toward him. Seeing the slight grin on her lips in the moonlight ignited his ire.

"What are you doing here, my lady?" he asked, his tone cold.

"I've been waiting for you to end your silly card game. I had thought you'd come back to the ball, but when you did not, I followed you here. Why are you avoiding me, Your Grace?"

That she used his title was telling. So she'd picked up on his displeasure perhaps, or she was playing off against him when he too had used her title instead of her given name.

"I'm simply finishing my drink before calling my carriage. The ball has bored me, and I find I no longer wish to be here."

Hurt flickered in her gaze and he cringed that he'd

possibly upset her somewhat with his words. Did he wish to injure her? Maybe, and he hated the fact that it was solely due to jealously. Having to share Darcy with others, when he wanted her only for himself, was not something he handled well, it would seem.

"So you weren't going to come dance with me? You were going to scuttle away instead?"

"I do not scuttle, madam." He pushed one of the red balls across the table, completely missing the other balls set out at the opposite end.

Darcy came toward him, running her hand along the side of the billiards table. "We haven't seen each other since the summer house. Are you angry with me?"

Yes, damn it, he was angry. Angry that he wanted her so much. Angry that she seemed immune to him. Angry that others claimed her time. He frowned. "It has been a busy couple of days."

"Of course," she said, coming closer still. "I'm sure being the Duke of Athelby is very demanding."

Was she teasing him now? "Let me escort you back to the ball, Lady de Merle. I'm certain there are many other gentlemen who are only biting at the bit to dance with you and wondering where you are."

"I think not." Darcy came to stand in front of him, and this time her finger ran across the front of his coat, up his lapels, then slid about his neck, playing with the hair at the nape of his neck. "I do not care to dance with anyone else but you, Duke."

"That did not look to be the case earlier, my lady."

She pouted and then chuckled, a seductive sound that went straight to his nether regions. "You are displeased with me, and it's because you're jealous. Well, well, well, I had not thought I'd ever see the day that the Duke of

Athelby would be so telling. And in front of a woman as well."

"I'm not jealous." *Liar.* Damn it, he was so jealous he could hardly see straight. The thought of her returning to the ball, dancing with others, had him clasping her hips and holding her firmly before him. "I'm not jealous," he repeated, in the hopes it would be true.

"I do not enjoy seeing you dance with others either, Cameron." She leaned up and kissed him, and unable to deny her anything, he returned in kind and gave himself up to the de Merle.

DARCY STEADIED her heart as Athelby took control of the kiss and turned it from a chaste peck to something so much more. A kiss that was molten, full of need and ownership, his of her and hers of him. Through the embrace she came to realize that there was no turning back from the feelings that they both raised in each other. And nor did she wish to.

For weeks now they'd teased, kissed and danced with each other in this game of seduction, but no more. Tonight, right at this moment, Darcy wanted Athelby with her whole body and soul, and blast it, she would have him.

He walked her backwards until her bottom hit the edge of the billiards table. Without hesitation, he picked her up and deposited her onto the green, velvety top. The kiss continued, demanding and hot, and she fumbled with his front falls, wanting to feel him, touch and stroke him, not have any article of clothing impeding her desire.

He gasped through the kiss when finally she freed his member, and with a long, slow caress left heat to pool between her thighs.

"I want you, Darcy. I cannot breathe for want of you."

He fumbled with her dress, any care long gone as they frantically tried to rid themselves of their clothes so they could both end this torturous game they played.

"I too." She wrapped her legs around his hips and pulled him against her. His hard member jutted out, and using her hand, she guided him into her, a delicious impalement that left her full, heady with need and completeness.

For a moment Athelby didn't move. His hot breath rasped against her neck, making her shiver.

"Ah, Christ, Darcy. You feel like heaven."

He was heaven as well, a torturous, exciting gentleman she couldn't get enough of. He didn't move, just remained still, and Darcy couldn't stand a moment longer of the inaction. "Rock into me, Cameron. Please."

The duke swallowed and meeting her eye he did as she asked, his thrusts slow at first, before becoming long and deep, meaningful and controlled. For a man who'd never had a woman before, he was certainly exceeding all her expectations.

Not only that, but he didn't seem to be slowing, or showing signs of not being able to last, as her husband was wont to do when they had shared a bed. No, Athelby clasped her bottom, pulled her more solidly into him and took her, pushing her toward a climax that she'd only ever reached by herself, or with this man over the last few weeks.

She clutched at his shoulders, and the mural on the ceiling caught her eye. It was of a woman and a man, lying on a bed of clouds and entwined much like she and the duke were right now. How fitting that they were in a room with such artwork and creating their own masterpiece. He slowed, placing small, delicate kisses up her neck before taking her mouth. "Show me what else we can do. I'm certain this is not the only way."

She chuckled and disengaged herself from him before sliding off the table. "Lie down on the settee, and I'll show you another way."

He threw her a devilish grin, and strode pant-less with not one iota of care to the settee. She caught glimpses of his tight derriere as his shirt moved as he walked. Possessiveness shot through her that the man before her was hers, no one else's to ever see in this way, no one else's to kiss and love.

Cameron was hers.

On the settee, his jutting cock stood upright, ready and willing for more lovemaking. Darcy came to stand beside him, taking in all his glory and wanting to prolong their night for as long as she could.

"Wrap your hand around yourself and stroke. I want to see you do it."

His eyes widened, but he didn't deny her request, merely did as she asked, and touched himself.

"Tell me, have you ever done this before?"

"No." He sucked in a breath, his other hand reaching out to wrap about one of her legs, pulling her gently toward him. "But since I've had you, from the moment we first kissed, I've woken up hard and longing to be with you every day. I've wanted to take myself in my hand and pump myself to completion if only to imagine it was you I was losing myself within."

"You don't have to imagine any longer." She leaned down and kissed the tip of his penis. He mumbled something unintelligible and just to tease him further, she took him in her mouth, sliding her tongue down his rigid length and tasting them both on her lips.

"You're killing me," he said, his hand coming to clasp her hair, making it further unravel.

Not that Darcy cared. She was long past caring if anyone saw or knew what they were about. So long as she had Athelby, the ton could go hang, and after tonight there was no doubt in her mind that he would agree to make her his mistress. For them to have a liaison without any strictures or rules on the other.

The thought of the Duke of Athelby being her lover sent a shiver of delight down her spine and unable to deny herself a moment longer, she gathered up her dress about her waist and straddled him.

His gaze turned molten as she lifted herself a little and then took him within her. With each delectable inch, the urge to moan, to cry out with the wonderfulness of it all, was hard to deny, and she bit her lip to stop herself.

"Fuck, Darcy. I had no idea of what I denied myself."

She rode him, supporting herself on his chest as she became the one in control of the speed, the depth, and angle of their lovemaking. It was wholly satisfying and increasingly hard to stop herself from riding him like a wanton. "Had I known the Duke of Athelby was a man of many hidden talents, I would have seduced you years ago."

THE PAIN WAS REAL, torturous, and so fucking good he wanted to cry out. Having Darcy atop him, riding him, pulling him toward climax while he was fully embedded in her, her hot heat licking his cock and dragging him along, was the best thing he'd ever experienced in his life. All the years he'd denied himself a woman. What had he been thinking? What sort of man lived a half-life due to such a choice?

He'd been bitter for so long, angry and alone, but now,

with Darcy, she'd shown him that there was more to life than duty, rules, and regulations. Not that he would allow them to stay as they were for much longer.

Oh no. Darcy de Merle would be his wife before the Season's end. She would be safely stowed in his life and bed and no one would ever touch her, mistreat her, or dance with her again. She was his, and he was hers.

Wholeheartedly.

I love you.

Never had he ever seen anyone so beautiful, so free, and giving themselves with abandonment to him. Wanting to look upon more of her he slipped her bodice down and freed her breasts. They rocked with the force of their love-making, and he clasped one, circling her nipple with his finger until it puckered.

"Yes. Touch me," she begged, laying her hand atop his, clasping her breast.

She leaned back a little and the movement pushed him toward climax. Oh, dear god, he wouldn't be able to hold himself back for much longer.

"Cameron. Yes!" she panted, a light flush crossing her cheeks. Her pleasure brought his forth, and it shot through him like a bullet. He moaned her name, leaning up and kissing her hard as he spilled his seed within her hot, wet core.

His breath was ragged, and he watched as slowly they regained their composure, although he was unwilling to move. If he had a choice, he'd never move again, so perfect was their current location.

"I fear, Lady de Merle, that I'm unable to live unless you're in my life."

Darcy clasped his cheeks, kissing him slowly and with such perfection that his cock twitched, wanting more of the same. More of her, a delicious morsel that he'd never tire of.

"I fear the very same thing, Duke."

Relief swam in his blood at her words. Tomorrow, first thing, he would gain a special marriage licence and make Darcy his bride. There wasn't a moment to lose.

CHAPTER 8

The following morning Darcy sat in her room and asked her butler to allow the Duke of Athelby to wait in the library while she finished her morning routine. He was unfashionably early, and she'd not thought to see him again until tonight at Lord Boulder's dinner.

She frowned as she came down the stairs. What was he about being here at this time? Did he regret last night? Maybe now that he'd had her and some hours had passed since she'd taken his virginity, he was rethinking his future with her.

She paused at the library door, swallowing the sickness that threatened to rise up. She did not wish for them to part, and she so hoped he would be open to being her lover. They did make quite a good pair, and after last evening, were more than compatible with each other.

The butler opened the door and she strode in, coming to a halt when she spied him beside the unlit hearth. Today he was the Duke of Athelby, regal, authoritative, serious, his clothing immaculate. His hair was combed back and in order. Not even his cravat would dare to be out of place today, it would seem.

His appearance was formal, and it gave her pause.

"Good morning, Your Grace. I hope I have not kept you long."

He shook his head, a flicker of trepidation passing through his eyes before he blinked and it was gone. "Not at all. And I apologize for coming so early, but what I have to say could not wait until the suitable at-home time."

"Of course," she said, coming to sit before him on the settee.

He started to pace before stopping and clasping his hands behind his back. "I'm sure you know why I have come here today?"

She smiled up at him, wanting to untie his cravat and ruffle his hair. He looked so severe and cross, nothing like the man who'd come apart in her arms the evening before. Not willing to let him stand before her in such a way, Darcy went over to him and wrapped her arms around his waist. "I believe I know why you're here, and it was something I was going to talk to you about this evening. When we had some time alone."

"You were?" he asked, clearly shocked but not pulling away from her impromptu hug.

"Yes, you wish to discuss the formalities of us becoming lovers, do you not? And I do not mean only when we're together at balls and parties, although those times are wicked fun, but here and at your residence as well. We will be discreet, I promise."

The duke stumbled back and clasped the mantle for support. "Clearly you jest."

"Jest? Why would I joke about such a thing? I mean, I do not know the rules of having a lover, of being some-one's mistress, but I do believe it requires us to not show open displays of affection, while being together quite often when alone. To partake in house parties and trips with our mutual friends so we can be alone."

The duke placed his arms behind his back, lifting his chin in a determined set. "I did not come here to ask you to be my mistress."

Despair made her knees weak, and she sank back onto the settee. "Then why did you come?"

"I came, Lady de Merle, to ask for your hand in marriage."

For a moment words failed Darcy and realizing she was gaping at him, she shut her mouth with a snap. "To be your wife!"

"Yes." The cold, determined word left her reeling.

"No." Her response wasn't at all filtered, and she cringed when hurt flickered through his eyes.

"May I ask why, madam, that me asking for your hand in marriage is so abhorrent to you?"

She clasped her hands in her lap and took a calming breath. "It's not abhorrent, but marriage is not an institution that I wish to be a part of again. My first marriage was a disaster and only diverted when his lordship decided to have a heart seizure beneath his whore. I do not want to be beholden to anyone, but I do wish to have a man in my life. To make love to him whenever I wish without having to promise to obey and honor him before God, when it is most likely, as I well know, that it's only the woman who has to abide by the rules."

"I am not Lord Terrance, Darcy. I would never dishonor you in such a way as to have a mistress."

"I have heard such declarations before, you know, and it did not make one ounce of difference when Terrance saw someone he wanted."

Athelby started to pace, and she steeled herself to be strong.

"Cameron, we can have a life together, be lovers and enjoy ourselves without marriage getting in the way. You said yourself only a few weeks ago that I was not suitable to be a duchess, and you are right. Nor do I wish to be."

The muscle at his temple jumped.

"Please don't be angry with me." Fear seized her that she may lose him. "I do want you, just not marriage."

"I cannot have a mistress, Darcy. It is bad enough that I have slept with you without taking vows before God. Over the last few weeks I have fallen under your spell, and I cannot remove myself from it. You know I am a man of rules and for doing what's right. Do not ask to be my mistress. I could not dishonour you so. I want you as my duchess. I'd like a wife. Children."

Tears pricked her eyes that she would hurt him. "I cannot be your wife. I will not be any man's wife ever again." She stood and went over to a decanter of whisky and poured herself a dram. "My marriage was horrible, truly awful, and Terrance has cured me of the ill wish."

Cameron stormed over to her, taking the glass from her hand and making her look at him. "I am not the earl, damn it."

She took the glass out of his hand and drank it down in one gulp. She would need all the alcohol she could get to tumble through denying her duke. "What you just did is why I'll never have another man think they own me. You do not get to choose what I want. You do not get a voice in what I'll do. If I wish to drink whisky at nine twenty in the morning, I damn well shall. And if I want to say no to your proposal, I shall do that as well." She hated hurting him, but the fear of marriage, of being owned, was too great, and she couldn't help herself. "I wish to be your lover, but that is all. Do not ask any more of me than that."

Athelby glowered at her, any pretence of not being angry with her long gone. In fact, she would easily surmise that he was furious.

"You could be carrying my child. Are you going to make an innocent babe a bastard simply because you do not wish to be a wife?"

The statement made her start. She'd not thought of such a possibility. "If I am increasing, which we shall know soon enough, I will marry you, without hesitation. I would never do that to a child, but we don't know that yet, and so as of this time, my answer is no."

"You stubborn woman." He stalked to the door and ripped it open. "Let me know via correspondence what the outcome of that possibility is, and we'll deal with it then. Until such time, good day to you, my lady."

"Cameron," she said, following him into the foyer. "Please try to understand my reasons. They were never put in place to hurt you. I would not wish to do that."

"And yet you have." He bowed. "Good day to you, madam."

She swiped at a wayward tear as the duke slammed the door in her face. She went to the window and watched him enter his carriage, that door too being slammed even though the coachman had been trying to close it with dignity.

His carriage pulled away, and the severing made her clasp her chest. Was it wrong of her to never marry again? Was she being selfish and cruel to a man who did not deserve to be tarnished with the same dark cloud as her husband?

Yes, the duke was opinionated, a nuisance when it

came to rules, but he was also passionate, caring, and wanted her to be his wife. Was she wrong in saying no?

She walked back into the library and sat before the unlit fire. That conversation had not gone at all as she'd planned upon seeing him here this morning. Never had she thought the duke ever wanted her, especially as a wife. So many times, he'd said she was too opinionated, too wild, like her family. Not to mention she was not a virgin, pure and sweet like so many gentlemen wanted to marry. She had been married to a man who cared not the briefest bit about her, who ruled her and made her obey him at every turn while living his life in the exact opposite way.

She rubbed her temples as a headache threatened. Not that Athelby was like that, but being so rule-abiding, how long before he turned into a mirror image of Terrance? Made her toe his line and not put a foot wrong. The wife of a duke had a lot more responsibility than an earl's countess, and Darcy did not care for it. No matter how much she cared for Cameron, as far as she was concerned the title could go hang.

For a time, she sat in the room before a maid entered and she requested tea. Pain tore through her that she'd pushed away the one man that she'd ever longed for, loved even, if she were honest. They were opposites, there was no doubt, but that opposition suited each other perfectly.

She thought over his brother's death and could understand his need to marry her. His brother had cared little for the fairer sex, had bedded many women, and had died in a reckless carriage race over his current lover, leaving many broken-hearted women in his wake.

Athelby's determination to not be like his sibling made him honourable and made her love him more than she thought possible. He'd stated he was not Terrance, and he'd proven that many times since they had been together.

He cared for her, loved her, and instead of asking her to be his mistress, he'd wanted her as his wife.

She swiped at another tear. What had she done? Her fear of rules had ensured she'd pushed away the man she loved. Maybe forever. Whatever would she do now?

IN THE WEEK since Darcy had denied him, Athelby had become a complete and utter dunce, and even he knew it. And yet he found it hard to alter his course. All too easily, he had reverted to the prim and proper duke, as so many called him—glowering at any person who dared to look happy, partook in a dance, or slipped even the slightest with etiquette.

He was an ogre, and he hated it.

After her denial of him, he'd spent the next few days in a haze of despair. Had even contemplated having her as his mistress and be damned to a wife. The life she asked for, where both were free to do as they pleased while coming together for pleasure, was appealing, and one night he'd almost knocked on her front door to beg her to do just that. Forget his proposal and have him in just the way she wished.

But the pain his brother had inflicted on the family, the scandal that had rocked a ducal line that had been a pinnacle of grace and dignity, could not be repeated again, and certainly not in his time. He could not do it.

The Marquess of Aaron came to stand beside him, throwing him an amused glance. "There are rumors afoot that you've won the bet at White's. Some are even saying you were seen in a highly scandalous embrace with Lady de Merle at Leeder's ball."

Athelby glowered at Hunter, if only to keep up the appearance that the notion he was the source of gossip did not rattle him to his core. Oh, dear god, had anyone seen them in the billiards room? He cringed and downed the last of his whisky, one of the vices he'd taken up that he did not wish to give up now that he'd started.

"As I said before, the betting book at White's can go hang."

Hunter chuckled, clapping him on his shoulder. "The source was a reliable one, and I'm sorry my friend, but he's a gentleman who's married to one of London's most gossiping tongues."

Sir Walton's wife.

Damn it. Athelby looked across the sea of dancers and met Darcy's troubled gaze. So she too was aware of what was being said about the ton.

"What are you going to do about the situation, my friend? You cannot leave de Merle to the wolves. After her previous marriage, she does not deserve to be ruined simply because you could not keep your hands off her."

The steely tone of Hunter's words fired his ire. "I asked her to marry me, if you must know."

Hunter choked on his wine, apologizing to a nearby matron who looked at him with distaste. "Well, I never thought I'd see the day."

"And nor will you, for she said no."

His friend had the good grace to look appalled before he laughed. In fact, the bastard threw back his head and bellowed over his misfortune. Athelby clenched his fists at his side lest one of them connected with the Marquess' jaw.

"I cannot believe it. The delectable Darcy de Merle turned down the Duke of Athelby. Whatever are you going to do about it?"

What could he do about it, save kidnap the lady and force her to marry him? Which of course was an absurd notion and not one that sat well with him. Kidnapping, no matter if you loved the person or not, was out of the question.

Too scandalous for starters.

"There is nothing to be done. I asked, she said no. Duke or not, I cannot force her hand."

"Do you want to marry her still?"

"Of course I do," he said without question or pause. He would marry her tomorrow if she would only say yes. But she did not want him in that fashion. Darcy wanted a lover, a temporary bedmate to pass the time. Not an annoying husband who curbed her freedom. Or so she thought.

"Will you share as to why she rejected your offer?"

Athelby met his friend's gaze. "She simply does not wish to marry again, and who could blame her after marriage with the Earl of Terrance? Never was there such a disgusting piece of flesh as he and his many whores."

Hunter whistled. "I gather you did not like the chap."

In truth, he'd always hated the man, the one reason more than any other being the simple fact he'd married Darcy. His grandmother was right about her. She was perfect for him simply because they were complete opposites.

He sighed. "I asked her to be my wife, and she asked me to be her lover. And you know Darcy's temperament, there will be no changing her mind."

"Show her you're willing to change. Maybe even be her lover for a time and win her that way. At least you'll be together."

Hunter made a good point and Athelby thought about it a moment. "I don't want a mistress, and I certainly know better than to make a de Merle one. I'd have her family down on my head and demanding retribution at dawn."

"True," Hunter said, pursing his lips. "They would not care for it on second thoughts."

He had that right, and as much as he wanted Darcy, he wasn't willing to make her his whore. It was certainly what being a mistress, in a liaison such as she suggested they have, would make her. And he did not want such an outcome. He wanted her to be his wife, his duchess. His everything.

"I will talk to her again. With the whispers about town over our indiscretion, it may make her open to negotiation and discussing the marriage option once more."

"I wish you well, my friend."

"Thank you," he said, and watched Hunter disappear into the crowd before heading toward Darcy. Coming up to her, he was pleased that the small group of women who had congregated about her dispersed.

She curtsied. He bowed. "Lady de Merle, please would you care to dance?"

Darcy raised one brow and watched him for a moment. He couldn't discern what she was thinking or even if she'd say yes. In fact, when she continued to remain silent he couldn't help but look about and see if others were watching their exchange.

He sighed, noting they were. "Please dance with me."

She shrugged and placed her hand atop his own and he led her onto the floor as the first strains of the waltz sounded. He pulled her against him. Her warmth and scent of roses intoxicated his soul and he fought not to clasp her too tightly, beg her to be his bride so they might never be apart again. Tell her that he'd never curb her exuberance for life.

She wouldn't meet his eye, simply stared over his shoulder. "I gather you wish to discuss something, Your Grace."

"I do. I'm sure you've heard the rumors that are circulating London about us."

"I have."

She said nothing more, and he wanted to shake some sense into her. Did she not know such a scandal could ruin her? As a man, a duke, there was no risk to him. Oh yes, some of the matrons of the ton might look down their noses at him for his indiscretion, but they would not dare cut him in society. Darcy faced the complete opposite, widow or no.

"And with the knowledge that if this story about us continues to gain momentum your reputation could be tarnished, ruined in this set, will you think on my offer some more? I know I'm not the easiest of men—I certainly have my opinions on matters pertaining to etiquette and rules—but I promise I shall try and make you happy, be a better husband than your last one. Give you all that you want and more." He was begging now, but he didn't care.

Darcy did look at him then, her paleness giving him pause. "Are you well?" he asked.

She shook her head. "I'm sorry, Athelby, but I cannot marry you. I do not wish to be bound by rules, marriage, and man. I want to be on my own, to do as I please whenever I please."

"You can still do that with me," he said, desperate to make her his. "You can do whatever you want, just be my wife."

"I may have seduced you, Duke, shown you another side of life, but who you are is ingrained in every ounce of yourself. I do not want anyone to change who they are just to please me. If you're not willing to be my lover, in a union such as where we promise fidelity for however long that may be, then after tonight we cannot meet like this again."

"So you'll cut me from your life should I not agree to make you my mistress?" Athelby's stomach clenched. "Be reasonable, Darcy. The rumor about us is true, you know that very well, not to mention the woman telling all and sundry is one of the ton's biggest gossipers. You'll be ruined."

"And if I am I'll return to my home in Devon, retire to a country life and travel. I do not need society, and I will not do what I'm told merely to save my reputation. I will not be owned by any man again. The last one was quite enough."

"I am not Terrance, surely you must see that." He pulled her to the side of the room, heedless of whoever noticed their hasty departure from the dance. "Marry me, please."

"Why are you so determined? I don't understand you."

He frowned. "Damn it all to hell," he said, ignoring the gasps about him. "I'm determined, Darcy de Merle, because I damn well love you—I think I have always loved you—and I want you. I want to shower you with everything that I am and own. I want to give you freedom if only you'll promise to return to me each night."

DARCY STOOD before the Duke of Athelby and could not form words even though hundreds of them bounced about in her brain, begging to come out. He loved her?

Butterflies took flight in her belly, and she clasped her abdomen. Had Cameron really just uttered those words, and before the ton?

Yes. Yes, he had.

It was certainly the most scandalous thing he'd ever done, in public at least, and it warmed her heart knowing that he'd declared himself so all could hear. To make her see how much he wanted her as his wife and not care who was about them.

How very rule-breaking that was.

Not that she was willing to let him persuade her so easily. The Duke of Athelby was against public displays of affection, against allowing couples to dance more than once when at balls and parties, and against many other things too numerous to mention. She laughed to herself. Athelby could've given her deportment teacher Miss Rivers a lesson or two, and Darcy had never thought to know someone as strict as that old biddy.

"You love me. Why?"

Athelby stood tall, placing his hands behind his back as if facing a set down from his peers, and yet he remained calm, his beautiful sharp features cajoling her to change her mind.

"I have always loved you, I believe, and yet it wasn't until you said 'I do' with Lord Terrance that I realized what I'd lost due to inaction. I may not have always loved your opinionated manners, your love of life, your honesty and loyalty to your friends, but I do now, so very much. I think your laugh is the sweetest sound on earth and your kisses the most wicked. I adore that when I'm with you, I forget myself, my rules and regulations, and just live." He stepped toward her, cupping her cheek. "Be mine and let me be yours. Please, Darcy."

Oh dear... Darcy swallowed and hoped her heart didn't pump out of her chest. People had stopped dancing and not a whisper could be heard as everyone in attendance watched the Duke of Athelby declare himself in the most public manner.

"If...and I have not agreed to anything as yet, Your Grace, but if I do, will you promise not to tell me what I can and cannot do? Will you promise me that if I wish to travel, visit friends abroad, that I shall be allowed to? That I will not be made to sit at home, alone night after night, while you while away your time at houses of ill repute? That you will love me, stay true to me from this day forward?"

He nodded, stepping closer still. "We shall put all those promises in our wedding vows."

Darcy smiled, hope making her eyes well up with tears. "Then yes, I shall be your wife."

Athelby laughed, his shoulders slumping in relief before he pulled her against him and kissed her. Devoured her would be a better term. Surprisingly, their public display of affection had the guests cheering and shouting congratulations while he kissed her still, held her steadfast against him and wouldn't let her go.

"Your Grace, I do believe you've forgotten yourself and where you are," the Marquess of Aaron whispered to them both.

Darcy chuckled and pulled away from the kiss but not Athelby's embrace.

"And what if he has? We're to be married, so what does it matter?"

Athelby went to speak, but Darcy placed her fingers over his lips, not willing to hear all the silly little tonnish rules they were breaking and who would be quite put out with them over the next few weeks and months. If anyone chose to be insulted by two people agreeing to love and marry one another then that was their problem and not hers to worry about.

"Shall we leave, Your Grace?" Darcy grinned, thoughts of them being alone in the carriage, of having Athelby in her bed for the rest of the evening, making her impatient to depart.

He tucked her arm into the crook of his and they made

their way across the ballroom floor. They stopped by Darcy's godmother and Athelby's grandmother, Lady Ainsworth, who was wiping away tears with her handkerchief.

"Oh, my dears, I'm so happy." Her ladyship kissed them both and clasped her hands before her. "I knew you were perfect for one another and I knew it was only a matter of time before you saw it yourselves."

Darcy looked up at Athelby and smiled. "How wise you were, Godmother. If only we were quicker to realize ourselves."

Others congratulated them on their way to the entrance hall. Darcy wrapped her cloak about her as they waited for Athelby's carriage to come around front.

"Is the Duke of Athelby's rule-breaking going to continue this evening?"

"What did you have in mind?" he asked, leaning down to whisper the words against her ear, causing a shiver to run down her spine.

"That you come home with me and warm my bed."

The duke's gaze burned with hunger and it spiked her own need. He stormed from the entrance hall and yelled for his vehicle to hurry up. Darcy grinned and followed. Oh yes, maybe the Duke of Athelby was up for some mischief after all.

CHAPTER 9

Athelby snapped the door to the carriage shut and wrenched Darcy onto his lap, taking her lips with a hunger that was as foreign and welcome to him as ever.

She kissed him back with passion, and his cock hardened, straining against his breeches. Darcy wiggled against him, and he could not wait to take her. He had to have her now.

Desperate to feel her, he ripped at her gown, pulling it out of the way as she came to straddle his legs. She was wet, so deliciously wet for him that he groaned as he ran his hand over her core, teasing, flicking, before slipping two fingers inside.

She moaned, her own hands busy untying his front falls. His phallus sprang into her hand, hard and heavy, and she teased him, wrapping her beautifully clever fingers around his member and sliding up and down.

"Fuck, Darcy," he gasped, pulling her atop him and impaling into her hot core. The carriage rocked along as he pitched into her. Their lovemaking was frantic, the carriage full of gasps, moans, and declarations for more, harder, faster, deeper…

Mine. Mine. The words reverberated in his mind. The woman in his arms was going to be his wife, his duchess. How the knowledge warmed his soul.

She rode him, took her pleasure, coming apart in his arms, and he soon followed her into bliss. To imagine endless nights and days to come, years of her beside him, attending events, balls, family obligations, while knowing always she was his made his eyes well. He blinked, not believing the Duke of Athelby would succumb to such emotions.

Darcy watched him, wiped a small tear that ran down his cheek and met his gaze. "I love you, Cameron, so very much. I'm so glad of that night where you finally kissed me. You said earlier that you believe you've always loved me. Well, I may have stated that I disliked your ways, your rules, but I've never disliked you. Deep down I've always wanted to know what you'd be like if I peeled off your layers, got to know you again, and then debauched you as I so longed to do."

He chuckled. "Debauched? I suppose yes, you've totally ruined me as I've ruined you. I love you, Darcy, so very much that I cannot see my way forward without you beside me."

"And you will not have to, for I'm going to be your wife, and will corrupt you even more and maybe even spoil you so you'll never be able to live without me again."

"Shall we put those declarations in our wedding vows as well? Best to start as we mean to go on."

Darcy smiled, kissing him with a sweetness that made him ache. "We shall."

EPILOGUE

Four years later

Darcy strolled toward the duke, who sat sprawled on the lawn of their London estate, their two children giggling and running about him every time he made a lunge to grab and tickle them until they couldn't take it any longer.

Their birth had not been easy, and she thanked God every day that even though they could not have any more, they were blessed with two delightful, happy, healthy children.

Darcy came up to them and clasped Henry from behind, whisking him into the air and making him squeal. "I've got you," she said, kissing him multiple times on his neck and cheek before putting him back down, where he resumed his game with his father. Darcy sat and pulled Henrietta onto her lap, cuddling her and giving her too her fair share of kisses.

"Are you having fun with Papa? I wanted to tell you that Cook has made up some ices for you in the kitchen, if you wish to have some."

The children squealed and ran off as if the devil himself was on their heels, their nursemaid not far behind.

"You scared the children away," Cameron said, leaning over and pulling her down to lie beside him.

Darcy lay over his chest, looking up at him. "I did, didn't I?" she chuckled. "Is it terrible of me that I don't feel the least guilt about that?"

"You're a minx, but then, I would not have it any other way." He pulled her up toward him and kissed her.

Darcy deepened the embrace, having been away all afternoon at house calls.

"Let's leave for Ruxdon early, and get out of London. I'm tired of the Season and all that we're obligated to do during it. If we go home, we can do as we please, and with summer not far away, maybe we could even take the children boating for a day."

Cameron rolled her onto her back, pinning her to the ground with one leg scandalously between her own. She gasped, clutching at his hair and kissing him again.

"We'll leave the day after tomorrow, but you're aware Grandmother will wish to come? You know she never likes to be separated from the children. She adores them so."

"I do not mind, and with her at Ruxdon it'll give us some time to be alone…" This time Cameron shifted fully on top of her and she gasped. "You cannot lie on me like this here. Someone may see us."

He was unmoved, except for one part of his person that was moving and growing at a very rapid pace. "What do you expect? The Duke of Athelby has been corrupted by a de Merle. There is no saving me now or halting my desires. You did say you wanted to know what it would be like married to a debauched duke."

"I did say that, didn't I?" She sighed and gave herself

up to kissing him, teasing him just as he liked. There were many things she now knew the duke loved, and in turn, she adored that she was the woman to give him love and pleasure. That he loved her in return and gave her the freedom that she'd so longed for.

He groaned, the kiss turning from sweet to molten when Darcy shifted beneath him, placing him directly at her core and not in the least backing away from his need.

"Upstairs, Duchess. Now." Cameron stood, pulling her to follow him.

She did, only too willingly. Marriage to a debauched gentleman did make for enjoyable afternoons. And an enjoyable life, actually.

Dear Reader,

Thank you for taking the time to read *To Bedevil a Duke*! I hope you enjoyed the first book in my Lords of London series.

I'm forever grateful to my readers, so if you're able, I would appreciate an honest review of *To Bedevil a Duke*. As they say, feed an author, leave a review! You can contact me at tamaragillauthor@gmail.com or sign up to my newsletter to keep up with my writing news.

If you'd like to learn about book two in my Lords of London series, *To Madden a Marquess*, please read on. I have included chapter one for your reading pleasure.

Tamara Gill

TO MADDEN A
MARQUESS

Lords of London, Book 2

She saved his life, but can she save him from himself?

Hunter, Marquess of Aaron, has the ton fooled. Outwardly he's a gentleman of position, with good contacts, wealth and charm. Inwardly, he's a mess. His vice—drinking himself into a stupor most days—almost kills him when he steps in front of a hackney cab. His saviour, a most unlikely person, is an angel to gaze at, but with a tongue sharper than his sword cane.

Cecilia Smith dislikes idleness and waste. Had she been born male, she would already be working for her father's law firm. So, on a day when she was late for an important meeting at one of her many charities, she was not impressed by having to step in and save a foxed gentleman rogue from being run over.

When their social spheres collide, Hunter is both surprised and awed by the capable, beautiful Miss Smith. Cecilia, on the other hand, is left confused and not a little worried by her assumptions about the Marquess and his demons. It is anyone's guess whether these two people from different worlds can form one of their own...

CHAPTER 1

Cecilia Smith stood on Curzon Street and tried to hail a Hackney cab. The streets were busy with coal carts, people walking along the cobbled footpath and gentlemen with their ladies out for an afternoon stroll. Cecilia pulled her spencer closed as a light breeze chilled the air, and waved to another Hackney that too, trotted past without a backward glance.

What was going on? Did they not see her? The thought was probably closer to the truth than she liked to admit. Here in Mayfair, in the drab, working-class gown that she was wearing, it was any wonder no one bothered to stop to pick her up. The working populace that was her sphere wasn't well-to-do enough for this locale, and it had not passed her notice that a lot of those out and about had thrown her curious, if not annoyed glances her way that she'd dared enter their esteemed realm.

From the corner of her eye, a flash of black arrested her attention. Turning to look, she observed as a gentleman stumbled toward a street lamp, leaning up against it as if it were the only thing keeping him upright.

He was a tall gentleman, his clothing was cut to perfection, and fit his tall, muscular frame well, but his eyes that she could see even from across the road were blood-shot with dark rings beneath them.

Was he ill, suffering apoplexy or merely drunk?

A hackney cab barrelled down the road and showed no signs of slowing. Cecilia turned her attention back to the gentleman and horrifyingly watched as he started across the busy thoroughfare.

Without a moment's hesitation she started toward him, and looking toward the hackney cab wasn't sure if even she would make it out of its way before it was too late. What an absurd, stupid man for putting himself and now her also in danger. Did these Mayfair dandies have no sense?

He stumbled just as she made his side, and heaving him with all of her might thumped him hard in the chest, sending him to flay backward and toward the safety of the side of the road. Unfortunately, he reached out at that very moment and brought her down with him. The man's head made a loud crack as it hit the cobbled pavement.

The hackney cab rattled past without so much as a by-your-leave and Cecilia scrambled to her feet and stood next to the man, peering down at him. The scent of spirits wafted from him, almost as if he'd bathed in the stuff and his uncertain footing and stupid attempt to cross the road without care was all too clear. Nevertheless, she couldn't just leave him there, even if she really wanted to. How lovely it would be to be able to prance about town at midday, drunk and without a care, as this fellow seemed to do. He must be one of those rich nobs that waltzed at balls and believed everything that was said or written about them was true.

If only they knew that her class laughed and mocked them at every turn. If it weren't for her kind, London would screech to a halt, no matter what the upper ten-thousand thought. They might make the laws, employ many, but it was her lot in life that kept the city running, and the country counties too when she thought about it.

He moaned, and she kneeled beside him, tapping his cheek lightly. His clothing smelt of stale wine, his breath reeked of spirits and a hard night, not to mention there was a slight odor of sweat that permeated the air. When he didn't respond to another gentle prod, she gave him a good whack. His eyes opened, his dark blue orbs wide in shock before narrowing in annoyance. This close to him, Cecilia noticed his sharp cheekbones, strong jaw and his too perfectly shaped nose was probably prettier than her own.

"What do you think you're about hitting me like that? Have care, miss, miss, miss."

She stood and held out her hand. He gazed at it in confusion before she sighed and leaning down again, took his hand in hers. "Stand, before you're nearly run over again by another carriage. And do be quick about it. I'm late for my meeting already."

He moaned as he allowed her to help him up. Cecilia led him onto the footpath and ensured he was well off the road before she let go of his hand. "Is your home nearby? Can I escort you there to ensure your arrival is to a satisfying end, unlike the one you almost had on the road just now?"

He frowned, rubbing his forehead. "I was on the road?"

"Yes, you were. Just how foxed are you sir?"

"I'm not a sir," He replied with an arrogant tilt of his head.

Cecilia took a calming breath to prevent herself from pushing the imbecile back onto the road. Really. Wasn't a sir? "Pray tell me, what are you then? I'm sure it's important that I must know to correct my silly ways?"

"Are you being sarcastic?" A small quirk turned his lips. Cecilia found her attention riveted on the spot and she vexed herself that she would be so pathetic as to look at his mouth at such a time.

"You are a smart one, sir."

"I would have you know, I'm the Marquess of Aaron, Hunter to my friends. Hunt for those of even closer acquaintance."

"Well, aren't we vulgar." Cecilia stepped away from him, dusting down her gown after their collision. "If you're safe and well enough to manage to get yourself home before you're struck by another vehicle I shall leave you now." Cecilia turned and started down the pavement. She left the marquess standing behind her, his agape mouth the last memory she'd have of him. She smiled a little, imagining he'd not been talked to so abruptly before. Not that he didn't deserve to be brought down a level or two.

"Wait!" he demanded, his footsteps hastened as he came up beside her. "You didn't tell me your name."

Since his lordship was so particular about titles, Cecilia decided to play a little trick on him. "I am the Duke of Ormond's daughter. Heir to a massive fortune and looking for a husband."

He started. "Really?"

"No. Not really. I'm Miss Cecilia Smith. My father owns and runs J Smith & Sons, Lawyers and I reside in Cheapside if you must know. I am also late for a charity meeting. So if you do not mind, I shall leave you to your stupor and go."

She moved on and ignored the light chuckle she heard behind her. He didn't follow, but she felt the heat of his gaze on her back. It was a pleasant feeling knowing he was watching her, not that she would ever see him again. Their social spheres were eons apart and he would only look to her Society for mistresses. Never marriage, unless it was absolutely necessary due to financial woes or some other such reason.

And as much as she hated to admit it, Cecilia had heard of the Marquess of Aaron and the wild and naughty antics the rich toff was known for around London. If what they wrote in the papers about him was accurate, he was a man who lived life fast and hard and left a bevy of young women pining for him to marry them. It was rumored that if he asked for a dance, they were instantly in love with him.

Cecilia rolled her eyes, not impressed by her first encounter with the gentleman. Waving again to a Hackney coming toward her, she sighed in relief when it pulled up, and she was able to travel the few blocks to her destination. The carriage rocked to a halt on the corner of Fleet Street and St Bride's Avenue. Cecilia stepped down from the carriage, paid the driver before turning her attention to the meeting at Old Bell Tavern where she wanted to press her idea for another orphanage and school on Pilgrim Street in Ludgate where a large, unoccupied building currently sat. Her father had promised her the funds, and now all she had to do was get the women at her meeting to agree and then all her plans would come to fruition. It was the right thing to do, and she was sure she wouldn't have any trouble getting them to agree.

If she managed to be instrumental in making just one of the orphaned children of London have a good stable job that enabled them to live a full and happy life, then her work at the charity was worth it. It was the best day in the world when children who'd arrived, sick and poor left and became house and ladies' maids, cooks even, if their inclination leaned them in that direction. The boys becoming footmen, stable hands and those who were mathematically inclined, stewards even. If one wanted to change, one had to work toward the goal and not believe everything would just fall in your lap.

With invigorated stride, Cecilia pushed open the doors at the Bell Tavern and headed for the private parlor where they always had their meetings. Life was excellent, and she was about to make it even better, especially for those who lived on the streets that had no life at all. Not yet at least.

Want to read more? Purchase To Madden a Marquess today!

KISS THE WALLFLOWER SERIES AVAILABLE NOW!

If the roguish Lords of London are not for you and wall-flowers are more your cup of tea, then below is the series for you. My Kiss the Wallflower series are linked through friendship and family in this four-book series. You can grab a copy on Amazon or read free through KindleUnlimited.

LEAGUE OF UNWEDDABLE GENTLEMEN SERIES AVAILABLE NOW!

Fall into my latest series, where the heroines have to fight for what they want, both regarding their life and love. And where the heroes may be unweddable to begin with, that is until they meet the women who'll change their fate. The League of Unweddable Gentlemen series is available now!

LEAGUE OF UNWEDDABLE GENTLEMEN

THE ROYAL HOUSE OF ATHARIA
SERIES

If you love dashing dukes and want a royal adventure, make sure to check out my latest series, The Royal House of Atharia series! Book one, To Dream of You is available now at Amazon or you can read FREE with Kindle Unlimited.

A union between a princess and a lowly future duke is forbidden. But as intrigue abounds and their enemies circle, will Drew and Holly defy the obligations and expectations that stand between them to take a chance on love? Or is their happily ever after merely a dream?

TO TEMPT AN EARL

TO VEX A VISCOUNT

TO DARE A DUCHESS

TO MARRY A MARCHIONESS

LORDS OF LONDON - BOOKS 1-3 BUNDLE

LORDS OF LONDON - BOOKS 4-6 BUNDLE

To Marry a Rogue Series

ONLY AN EARL WILL DO

ONLY A DUKE WILL DO

ONLY A VISCOUNT WILL DO

ONLY A MARQUESS WILL DO

ONLY A LADY WILL DO

A Time Traveler's Highland Love Series

TO CONQUER A SCOT

TO SAVE A SAVAGE SCOT

TO WIN A HIGHLAND SCOT

Time Travel Romance

DEFIANT SURRENDER

A STOLEN SEASON

Scandalous London Series

A GENTLEMAN'S PROMISE

A CAPTAIN'S ORDER

A MARRIAGE MADE IN MAYFAIR

SCANDALOUS LONDON - BOOKS 1-3 BUNDLE

ABOUT THE AUTHOR

Tamara is an Australian author who grew up in an old mining town in country South Australia, where her love of history was founded. So much so, she made her darling husband travel to the UK for their honeymoon, where she dragged him from one historical monument and castle to another.

A mother of three, her two little gentlemen in the making, a future lady (she hopes) and a part-time job keep her busy in the real world, but whenever she gets a moment's peace she loves to write romance novels in an array of genres, including regency, medieval and time travel.

www.tamaragill.com
tamaragillauthor@gmail.com